THE BOOK MINE

Koni

The Story of a Champion

Moti Nandy (1931–2010) was one of the few writers in the world to have created an entire body of fiction centred on sports. A Sahitya Akademi award winner, this former Sports Editor at the *Ananda Bazaar Patrika* wrote more than 25 novels in Bengali for adults and as many for children and young adults. His novels—almost all of them set in Kolkata, where he lived—capture the life, struggle and success of the underdog in sports ranging from football to cricket, tennis to swimming, athletics to boxing. Of all his writings, *Koni* was made into a film starring Soumitra Chatterjee, and won the National Award for Best Film in 1985.

Sumana Mukherjee spent the first 25 years of her life in Kolkata and has since lived in five cities across India, working as a journalist and writing on subjects she loves most: books, food and travel.

MOTI NANDY

Koni
The Story of a Champion

Translated by Sumana Mukherjee

Introduction by
SRIPARNA MUKHERJEE

hachette
INDIA

First published in Bengali in 1975
This translation first published in 2010 by Hachette India
An Hachette UK company

www.hachetteindia.com

SRD

ISBN: 978-93-80143-55-2

Hachette Book Publishing India Pvt. Ltd
4th & 5th Floors, Corporate Centre,
Plot No. 94, Sector 44, Gurugram - 122003, India

Typeset in Goudy Old Style 11.5/15.5 by
Eleven Arts, New Delhi

Printed and bound in India
by Manipal Technologies Limited, Manipal

FSC
www.fsc.org
MIX
Paper from
responsible sources
FSC™ C104740

{Introduction}

Moti Nandy's novel *Koni* was published much before the film based on it was made. His story was a very moving one, and his depiction of a poor—and often hungry—but determined girl, and of the swimmers' world was very authentic and touching. I had read the book, and had always regarded it a powerful classic. It inspired me just as much as it would inspire anyone and everyone working towards a goal.

Let me now go back to the backdrop of how events started to unfurl and I ended up acting in *Koni*.

As a child I suffered frequently from cold and cough, and a doctor advised my parents to teach me swimming. What began because of medical advice, turned into a passion for me. By the time I was twelve, I was winning races, and never looked back. In the 1970s I became a national winner, and was national swimming champion Nafisa Ali's contemporary. I held the national open record in breaststroke. I became well-known in swimming circles, and perhaps that's why my name came up when the film's producers were casting for the character of Koni.

By the time the film project began, I was in Jadavpur University, studying International Relations. I was delighted when I came to know that the film's producers were even considering me for the role. However, Saroj Dey, the director, had one look at me and didn't like me at all—he thought I looked too 'elitist', and he wanted someone with the lean, hungry, deprived look that would fit the part. They went in search of someone who was 'darker' (they didn't want to use make-up at all, to start with), and someone who had more of a poverty-stricken, struggling look. Though the idea of acting was attractive to me, my father was very conservative and didn't want me to do it. So that was that. And I thought the matter ended there.

For two years or so after they first contacted me, I didn't hear anything from the movie's producers. However, perhaps I was destined to be Koni. For two years later—and by then I was in my third year at the University—they came back. They had been persuaded by Jayant Bhattacharya, who was on the film-making team and had liked me in the first go. By that time they must have tried all sorts of actors, with swimmer doubles, and so on. There were problems with funding for the film—and the film started to be made only a year and a half later. The highlight was that even Soumitra Chatterjee, the well-known actor who played my coach in the film, came to our house. My father got persuaded as well, and so the shooting began.

I was determined not to disappoint anyone in the endeavour of essaying the role of Koni, since I had yearned for this role from the beginning. Koni's struggle was—is—one of dogged grit; when it would flag, her coach's faith would take over and drive her to go faster, stronger, farther. She won as much for him, and she did for herself. I realized I would have to bring that particular trait out in my character.

I worked hard to look like an absolute have-not. This began with my purchasing a really cheap dress, worth all of 12 rupees. The next stage was to mop the house with it, to produce a remarkably rag-like effect! I began to observe the lady who worked in our house, and tried to emulate the characteristics of the downtrodden. Long hours were spent at the clubhouse to get tanned deeply when the sun was shining at its mightiest. Slowly I would evolve into the desired character. So much so that for one scene—when we were shooting at the ghat on the Ganga, a huge crowd gathered. The police was called to keep the people under control. I was told to stay behind the ropes and come down the steps and past the rope for the shot. But no! They were not going to let me back in, mistaking me as one in the crowd. I kept smiling to myself thinking that the entire get-up was really good.

We went to the film shoot every day and loved it. The crew members were very informal. I knew all the other swimmers; all the girls who were my competitors in the film were my swimmer friends. It felt like going for a great big picnic. We were awestruck to come in such close contact with Soumitra Chatterjee, the incredibly talented actor who alone was the reason to bunk uncountable number of classes, to go to watch his movies. I remember him as a great personality, unspoiled by fame, showing immense dedication for his work. He broke the monotony of the shooting by mellifluously bursting into song and poems, and made the entire episode a memorable experience filled with fun, laughter and learning.

I had always swum in still waters earlier. I had never swum in a river or a sea where the current was very strong. Also, in a pool the light is totally different—

you can see underwater—but in the river it is dark and depthless. Both the strong current and the dark underwater frightened me a bit, but I was so keen to do the role that I would have done anything. That was my goal at that time, and my struggle, compared to the girl in the story, was small.

The film released in 1984 and went on to win me the Bengali Film Journalists' Association (BFJA) Best Actress Award, with the film winning the Golden Lotus. It won the National Award for Best Film as well. *Koni* was to be my one and only film. I am currently a teacher at South Point School in Kolkata.

Though Koni is a story about a poor girl, but it is meaningful for everyone. Any sportsperson, or for that matter a student, will understand the importance of a coach, a teacher, who believes in you so completely that you feel you can do it, that you can fight—and win.

The coach's exhortation, 'Fight, Koni, fight', became a popular phrase, oft-repeated, and has stayed with me. It will inspire everyone—young or old—who struggles to achieve a dream.

Kolkata, June 2010 Sriparna Mukherjee

{1}

Today was Baruni, a bathing festival. The Ganga was dotted with raw mangoes.

The ghats were packed with people, mostly elderly. They were taking a dip with the tiny raw mangoes balanced on their heads and letting them float away as an offering. Others flung the fruit away from the banks.

Small gangs of boys waited to collect the mangoes. Some of them stood neck deep in the river, others treaded water some distance away. A single mango triggered a rush. Two or three of them targeted the fruit, screaming, shouting and splashing water. Whoever managed to grab one, stored it in his pockets till they couldn't hold any more. Then he would come out of the water and hide the mangoes away somewhere in the ghats. No-one had the gall to touch them. Later, they would sell the mangoes dirt-cheap by the roadside.

Because of the low tide, the Ganga was shrinking away from the ghats. A muddy stretch lay between the steps (with the paved slopes on either side) and the river. Exasperated bathers had to negotiate the clayey mud before they could get to dry land. Then they would head towards the entrance to the ghats, where Brahmins took charge of clothes for a fee, provided mustard and coconut oils and painted sandalwood tikas on the forehead. The majority ignored the beggars lined up on one side of the road, while some didn't.

Then, most of them headed home, sprinkling Gangajal from their pots at the small temples of various gods and goddesses, and on the Shivlings on either side of the road. The temples gave way to shops stocking wood, plastic and iron goods, toys and household essentials. Some, perhaps, stopped to shop for vegetables at the street markets. Then, with the sun roasting the road, they walked home quickly with bare feet and bad tempers.

Lying supine on a ragged, oil-stained rush-mat for a massage, Bishtucharan Dhar was looking out over the Ganga. He was also in a bad temper.

Bishtu Dhar, popularly known as Beshtada, was a high-school graduate. He came from an aristocratic lineage, owned around seven houses and a business in Burrabazar, and most importantly, a 111-kilo body. A trusty Austin, as old as Bishtu Dhar at forty, carried him everywhere.

The cause of Bishtu Dhar's ill temper was a man about 30 feet away. Dressed in a white lungi and a saffron kurta, and carrying a colourful bag on his shoulder, he was looking his way and smiling mischievously. Bishtu knew that the man was laughing at his girth. When children laughed at him like that, Bishtu felt upset and wished he were thinner.

But this man was no child. He wore thick glasses, and his cropped hair was a mix of salt and pepper. Give or take five years, he was around 50 years of age. His complexion was a dusty terracotta. And his eyes!—the pupils looked like they had faded from black to gray by staring at the sun in a challenge. The look in his eyes suggested that anything that didn't agree with him could be blowtorched into submission. His jaws were clamped together stubbornly.

The masseur caught hold of Bishtu's waist and used his right knee to rapidly pummel his backbone, right up to the shoulder and back. After 10 rounds, he folded his hands in a namaste and used it like a shovel on Bishtu's back.

Then Bishtu tried to turn on his back and failed. It took the masseur several attempts to help him turn around. Gathering his towel into place, Bishtu gravely instructed, 'Play the tanpura.'

The masseur used all 10 fingers to grab, pull and release the gobs of lard all over Bishtu's body.

'Now the tabla.'

The masseur played the drums all over Bishtu's torso. Heaving a sigh of pure pleasure, it occurred to Bishtu that that man must be laughing aloud at the sight. His good mood evaporating, he said, 'Now the sa-re-ga-ma.'

Right away, the masseur began playing the harmonium

all over Bishtu's body. As his ticklish fingers crawled across the quivering masses of fat, Bishtu heard muffled laughter.

'Hey, what's so funny?' Bishtu said, lying on his back, staring up at the sky.

After about 20 seconds, Bishtu got the reply. 'Is this a massage or a music lesson?'

'Whatever it is, what business is it of yours?'

'Ever checked your blood pressure?'

'Why should you be interested?'

'What about your blood sugar? Cholesterol?'

'Who are you, mister, to ask so many unsolicited questions? Just have your bath and go.'

'That I will. But my guess is that your heart won't be able to pull around this mountain much longer.'

'What did you say!'

To sit up, Bishtu Dhar first leaned on his elbow and raised his head. Then he heaved himself up on his hands.

The man said meekly, 'At the same time, it's true I've never heard of an elephant or a hippopotamus suffering a coronary attack. So maybe I'm wrong.'

Too angry to talk, Bishtu Dhar stared daggers at the man, who began undressing down to his shorts.

Finally, Bishtu Dhar spluttered, 'I don't know what to say to you.'

'My wife tells me the same thing.'

'You are a nuisance.'

'Many people at my club say that as well.'

'Someone like you should be whipped black and blue.'

The man looked at him and smiled mischievously, like a child. 'Tell me, if I cuffed you on the head and ran away, would you be able to catch me?'

No sooner were the words out than the man began jogging on the spot. A lot of people stared at him; some thought he was bonkers.

Bishtu was stunned. Without warning, the man began jogging towards him with his hand upraised, as if he might hit out. Bishtu ducked. The man passed him by.

'Would you be able to catch me, huh? Remember, I'm older than you are.' The man was jogging back towards him. Bishtu Dhar stood up, huffing and puffing like a wild ox. At that, the man came to a standstill. Then he began swinging like a pendulum, left to right. Bishtu waited, his hands raised like two fat paws. The scene drew quite a few onlookers.

'I exercise every day,' the man told Bishtu. 'Isometrics, calisthenics, barbells—every single day. It works up an enormous appetite. Do you ever have an appetite?'

Bishtu Dhar didn't say a word; he only grunted.

'When you're ravenous, everything tastes heavenly. Have you ever had that pleasure?' Without waiting for an answer, the man jogged down the steps and then ran up again.

After three rounds on the steps, the man, panting now, came to a halt five yards away from Bishtu Dhar, who was now looking at him helplessly. His anger had been replaced by curiosity. In his mind, he had begun to exchange his obesity with the man's slim frame.

'I have no soft spot for food; I diet,' Bishtu announced grandly. Pride was evident in his tone.

The man came closer. 'What sort of a diet?'

'Earlier I ate half a kilo of kheer everyday, now I have 300 grams. I used to snack on 20 luchis, now it's down to fifteen. Rice is measured out strictly—just 250 grams. And 12 rotis at night. Almost no ghee at all—not a drop more than four spoons with steaming hot rice. In the afternoon, two glasses of sugar-candy juice and four pieces of sandesh. I don't touch meat or fish—we worship Radha-Gobindo at home. And I come here once a week for a massage. I'm not greedy you know—I can control my appetite. I'll never get heart disease; there's no history of it in my family. My father died of cholera after eating 70 deep-fried snacks, and my uncle died due to acidity.'

'Such self-control! How do you survive?' The man came forward and patted Bishtu Dhar's stomach.

'Oooh, that tickles.' Bishtu Dhar removed his hand, then added dolefully, 'My wife says the same thing. From morning till night, I look after my business. I deal in mustard, sugar, dal, many things. So much work, so little to eat! And to top it all, the humiliation.'

Seeing the man put out his hand again, Bishtu retreated a step. 'No, that tickles.'

'Who humiliated you?'

'Why, didn't you call me a hippo and an elephant! Did you think I'm so uneducated that I wouldn't get it?'

'No, no, I never said you're uneducated,' the man began cleaning his glasses embarrassedly. 'Actually, your weight is very dangerous for your heart.'

'Dangerous, meaning?' Bishtu Dhar tried to ask the question lightly, but it came out fearful. 'Will I die?'

'Yes, you might. Alternatively, you'll survive a few years, battling diseases and self-control,' the man replied, bending like a bow to touch his toes and straightening up again. 'You are four thousand times richer than I am, but even if you spend four lakh rupees, you'll never be able to make a slave of your body.'

'What do you mean!'

The man held his right elbow to his body and pitched his arm forward as if he was holding a pistol.

'Try pulling my arm down.'

Bishtu Dhar looked disbelievingly at the arm. Veins, arteries and knots stood out in the dry rootlike limb.

'Go ahead, pull it down.'

Bishtu clamped his fat fingers on the man's wrist and yanked. It didn't budge a centimetre. Bishtu bit his lips and wrenched harder. The hand remained where it was. Now Bishtu pulled down with all his might. Beads of sweat appeared on his forehead. A few people had gathered around them. They looked on intrigued, whether at the man's triumph or Bishtu's failure, it wasn't clear. Bishtu glanced up at the man to see a thin smile and mischievous eyes. He finally gave up, sighing heavily.

'How did you do that!'

'Strength doesn't mean only physical strength. Mental strength is all important. Willpower can make up for physical weaknesses. It can push the body to do much more than the body thinks it can. For that, one needs to train the mind, not just the body. The mind can command the body to do anything. Your mind doesn't know how to command, which is why your body couldn't do its bidding.'

Bishtu Dhar looked on dejectedly, muttering, 'I wish, I really wish I could be thin.'

Just at that moment, a shrill cry came floating from the banks of the Ganga. 'Koeeeeee-neeeeeeee. Koeeeeee-neeeeeeee.'

The man looked out over the Ganga.

{2}

A mango was bobbing along the Ganga. Three swimmers were chasing after it. Two or three 14-year-olds were standing in waist-deep water and cheering them on. The three were swimming neck-and-neck, their heads moving from side to side, their arms as stiff as paddles.

Suddenly, one of them began advancing, leaving the other two behind. Immediately, the cry rose: 'Koeeee-neeeeee, Koeeee-neeeeee.' The two laggards, too, increased their pace.

The mango was nearly within the boy's reach. Abruptly, he stopped. He was flinging his arms, but wasn't moving ahead. His head disappeared under water a couple of times. Then he began screaming in rage, kicking the water violently.

In the meantime, one of the other two had bagged the mango.

'One of them held his leg down,' said Bishtu Dhar.

The man laughed, took off his glasses and placed them in his bag. Depositing the bag with one of the Oriya Brahmins at the entrance to the ghats, he began to climb down the steps carefully. Without his glasses, he could have well been blind.

The three of them were fighting in the mud at the edge of the river, one against two, splattering the sludge all over. People moved away, grumbling. Two or three boys egged them on.

'Go on, hit him, go on, harder!'

Moulded in mud from head to toe, a reed-thin figure was flailing long arms about wildly. The other two were lurking just beyond that dangerous arc of the arms, looking for their chances.

'Fight, Koni, fight. Keep it up.'

One pounced on the other from the back. Both of them fell down.

'Hey, hey, Bhadu, no pulling Koni's hair. Do that and we'll throw a few punches too.'

Bhadu, seated on Koni's back, let go of the hair and tried to rub his opponent's face into the mud. Legs thrashing, Koni tried to sit up and then, without warning, wrenched Bhadu's right hand and bit down hard on two fingers.

Bhadu leapt up, screaming. Immediately Koni rose and turned on him. 'I'll gouge your eyes out—where's the mango? Dunking me! I'll bury you alive in this mud. Either you give me the mango or I'll scratch your eyes out.'

As the 10 curled fingers swooped down like an eagle's talons towards the prostrate Bhadu, two boys dragged Koni away.

'Let me go, Chandu, let go, Kanti! I have to get even. Dunking me!'

Koni was frothing at the mouth, snarling dangerously. The thin body swayed back and forth like the hood of a cobra.

'Bhadu, that mango is Koni's. Give it to her, otherwise you may just get your eyes scratched out!'

Bhadu was examining his right hand. He shuddered, 'It's bleeding! The teeth drew blood.'

Letting Koni go, Kanti came and dug into Bhadu's pockets. He brought out a few raw mangoes, selected the largest and threw it at Koni.

Koni caught the fruit, bit into it and grimaced. 'It's so tart! How can they offer Ma Ganga such stuff!'

Chucking the mango into the river and spitting out the mouthful, Koni came up to Bhadu. 'Let me see where I drew blood.'

Grasping his hand and looking closely at the fingers, Koni frowned. 'What rubbish, it's nothing. Come on, let's go back into the river. You deserved what you got; now you know what happens if you annoy me.'

* * *

After a few dips in the river, the man was scrubbing his back with a gamchha. He overheard an old man mumbling to himself: 'These kids will be the death of us. They ruin the ghats. They collect the mangoes dedicated to the river, and then they go and sell them. And now there's actually a tomboy with them! Why don't her parents say something!'

The man was going in for another dip when he stopped short. 'Who's the tomboy?'

'What do you mean—you haven't seen her? You do have a pair of eyes, don't you?'

The man turned to look. Without his glasses, all he saw was a hazy Koni fighting with Bhadu. Through the coating of mud, something of a girl seemed to flash through. The cropped hair clung to the skull. The tee-shirt, tucked into the trousers, stuck to her like a second skin. A tall, thin body. Scrawny arms, scrawny legs. The man couldn't make out if Koni was a girl or a boy.

One wave, and then another slammed against the man. Bishtu Dhar had waded into the water.

'Er, this business of making the body your slave, what exactly does it mean?'

'It's simple. Bite into iron, order the body to digest it, and your intestines will. Demand to be walked five miles and your feet will take you there. If you want to swing from a tree, your arms will obey.'

The man came out of the water and walked gingerly to the steps. Rinsing his gamchha, he looked out over the river. The ghats were crawling with people. It was impossible to make Koni out among them.

Dressed in dry clothes, bag on his shoulder, the man returned to the head of the steps, polishing his glasses. After returning them to his nose, he suddenly spotted four black specks in the heart of the Ganga. They had already crossed a quarter of the river.

'Koni,' the man said to himself. 'Koeee-ni.'

After staring at them for a while, he tied up his wet *gamchha* like a turban and made his way homewards.

Fifteen minutes later, the man entered a tiled single-storeyed house in a narrow lane. Directly beyond the front door was a courtyard that could just about accommodate a volleyball court. A number of plants and creepers—chillies, papaya, hibiscus, pumpkin and more—occupied the courtyard. On one side was the tin-roofed kitchen and bathroom, on the other was a verandah and, beyond that, two rooms. Surrounded by tall buildings on four sides, the one-storeyed house crouched peacefully in the middle. Haladhar Bardhan, the owner of the house to the north, had sent a couple of feelers to buy this one, but the man—with only a wife, Lilabati, and two cats to call his family—had declined politely.

The house received a limited supply of water. Lilabati liked using water, just as she liked having cats as pets. So the man frequently had to draw water from the public tubewell for his bath. This morning, though, the tubewell had run dry—which was why he had gone down to the Ganga after ages, for a dip.

He was putting up his trousers to dry in the courtyard when a short, plump figure emerged from one of the inner rooms. It was Bhelo.

'Kshid-da, I've been waiting for you for a while, and guarding the house, too. Someone came from the shop to call Boudi. She said she'd be back in just a while but—'

'Bhelo, make a quick cup of tea first.'

'What if Boudi comes!'

Kshid-da, alias Kshitish Sinha, thought for a couple of seconds and said, 'Then let it be. What brings you here?'

'Will you go for the meeting at the club today?'

'Of course, I will. Those boys won't work hard, won't be disciplined, won't do anything but play around in the pool. What's wrong in wanting them out of the club? Does anyone even spare a thought for that? And if Kshitish Sinha says something, they immediately call a council meeting.'

'You know that's not the reason—actually, Haricharan and his cronies nurse a grudge against you. They are the ones who instigated Shyamal and Gobindo to bring those charges against you.'

'That I know. Haricharan has wanted to be the chief trainer for a long time now. He told me as much last year. I'd told him, "Hari, you can't create a champion just by taking care of his diet and training. You have to understand his mindset and temperament, and guide him accordingly. A trainer has to be a psychologist, which means applying common sense. The mentor has to earn the respect of the protégé. He has to nurture his ambition through everything he says and does. He has to motivate him. You can't do all that. You simply rage at them and abuse them to make them work hard—you can't be the chief trainer."'

'Kshid-da, you need to drop this bad habit of lecturing everybody. What was the point in telling Haricharan all that? Anyway, you mustn't go to the meeting today—they plan to humiliate you.'

'If they want to, they will.' Kshitish picked up Bishu, who was rubbing his head vigorously against his leg, and scratched his neck. Bishu closed his eyes contentedly and began to purr.

'So you're determined to go!' Bhelo said, hitching up his trousers and raising his voice.

Kshitish, heading inside, answered indistinctly, 'Yes.'

Right then, Lilabati Sinha came into the house. A tiny, fair, serious woman, with slippers on her feet and an umbrella in her hand. She looked from one to the other, then addressed Bhelo, 'It's quite late—have lunch with us.'

Bhelo suddenly came back to earth. Glancing at the clock, he said agitatedly, 'No, Boudi, oh, it's so late. They'll be waiting for me back at home. I have to go now. Kshid-da, I do think it would be better if you stay away.'

As soon as Bhelo left, Lilabati asked Kshitish, 'What did he mean—that it would be better if you didn't go?'

'There's a meeting at the club today. He says there's a plan afoot among some of them to insult me so that I leave the club.'

'Oh, that would be nice. You're so obsessed with the club, you have no time for the business. I'm a woman, but I have to look after the shop. Just as well that we have no kids. I'd be so relieved if the club throws you out.'

Lilabati went into the kitchen. A forlorn Kshitish sat in the landing, absently fondling Bishu. Just then Khushi came out of the room, stretched, yawned and then deliberately walked towards the kitchen, holding her bushy black tail upright, sparing only a glance for Kshitish.

'Here, come on in,' came the summons from the kitchen.

Kshitish sat down to lunch, looking uncharacteristically grave. It was a simple meal, mostly boiled. Saving money or time or labour wasn't the point here. Kshtish believed that the typical Bengali meal was not healthy. It ruined the stomach and weakened the body, which was why Bengalis couldn't do much in any sporting arena.

Boiled food preserved most of the nutrients, proteins and vitamins.

Initially, Lilabati had rebelled at being denied the opportunity to use her spices—mustard, red chillies, cumin, coriander, panchphoran. But a furious fight and a three-day hunger-strike failed to change Kshitish's mind. He stuck to his conviction: 'The body will get used to whatever you subject it to.' Finally, Lilabati was permitted to use mustard and chillies one day of the week, that too only for her own meals. Kshitish never accepted invitations to social do's. He often told the children at the club:

'Dr. Roy, the revered chief minister of West Bengal, used to say that each wedding dinner takes a year off your life. Truer words were never spoken.'

Kshitish finished his meal without uttering a word.

Lilabati knew he was angry. She asked, 'Why will they throw you out? What have you done?'

Kshitish retorted with a question: 'Why did you need to go to the shop?'

The shop occupied a tiny sliver of a room along the tram tracks on Grey Street. It was called 'Prajapati'. Earlier, it was called 'Sinha Tailoring'. Two tailors ran up shirts and trousers; they also stocked some synthetic fabric. Kshitish used to manage the shop at that time, but he was hardly ever around. Apart from the afternoons, all his time was spent at Jupiter Swimming Club. Then, one day, he discovered that half the fabric had disappeared from the cupboards, four months' rent was pending and the business was making more losses than money.

That was when Lilabati stepped in and took charge. She employed two women with diplomas in tailoring, pawned her jewellery to do up the shop and renamed it 'Prajapati'. She stopped taking orders for menswear and began to tailor dresses and blouses for women and children. Within four years, Prajapati had spread its wings. Previously, they could turn out blouses in three days, now they needed at least ten. Lilabati had already got back half of her jewellery.

'We are cramped for space, so I'm looking for a bigger room.

I've heard of one near the Hatibagan crossing–it belongs to a client of ours. The lady of the house came to us for her daughter's clothes. That's why I had gone over for a chat.' Lilabati pulled forward Kshitish's plate and served herself rice and dal.

Kshitish had strong objections to Lilabati's eating off his plate. 'Unhygienic,' Kshitish had argued, 'These superstitions are the downfall of the Bengal.' Lilabati had replied extremely dispassionately, 'This is my business, don't worry about it.' Kshitish had realized immediately that if he prolonged the argument, it would bring about his own downfall. But he continued to register his opposition by refusing to be around while Lilabati ate.

On the bedroom walls, pictures of Kshitish's parents, a meditative Mahadev, and Krishna-Arjun at Kurukshetra hung next to magazine cut-outs of a medalled Don Schollander and a victorious Dawn Fraser. Besides which, there was the usual furniture–a bed, cupboard, boxes and other household things. In the next room, there was nothing apart from books and magazines, a wooden cot, and tucked underneath, training equipment: rubber ropes, springs, weights. Kshitish napped here for an hour every afternoon. There was no fan here, no bedding. He believed that not just the protégé, but also the mentor had to lead a Spartan life to create a champion. But of course, he didn't have a protégé.

Lying down on the cot, Kshitish sighed deeply. A protégé!

Just before he dozed off, Kshitish's subconscious drew a picture of two long arms, rising and falling like a pair of oars in the Ganga.

It faded, giving way to another image: A thin, spindly body encased in mud, as lethal as a hooded cobra, throwing about her long arms any which way. 'Fight, Koni, fight.'

Before dozing off, Kshitish mumbled incoherently, 'Koeee-ni'. Possibly, he had taken a fancy to the name.

{3}

Covered with a cloth, the table-tennis board did double duty for the meeting. Seven people sat around it. One place was vacant. Those present were talking to each other in low voices. Outside the room, a few youths loitered about, as if they were waiting for someone.

Binod Bhar, the new president of Jupiter Swimming Club and MLA, leaned to his right and asked the secretary Dhiren Ghosh, 'Is there just one item on the agenda? Or more?'

Dhiren Ghosh extended his long neck as far as he could to study the sheet of paper on the table, through the lower section of his bifocals. 'There's one main item. The rest is unimportant.'

'Do we have a quorum?'

'Yes, everyone's present.' Dhiren Ghosh bestirred himself. 'Jogu, tell them to serve the tea and sweets.'

Jogeshwar Bhattacharya had just about stood up, when the door opened. Kshitish Sinha ran an eye over everyone present and greeted them before lowering himself into the empty chair facing the president.

Jogu looked questioningly at Dhiren Ghosh, who nodded and said, 'Bring it in a little later.'

'I got late,' Kshitish smiled faintly at the president.

'Not really, just about four minutes.' Binod Bhar looked at his watch and then at Dhiren Ghosh. 'I'm actually in a bit of a hurry.'

'Of course, we're just about to start. There's nothing that should take up much time, except the swimmers' letter. And that's already been circulated, so there's nothing new to add.'

'Yes, there is.'

All heads turned towards Kshitish.

'The letter does not spell out the charges against me. I want to know what they are.'

Everyone looked at everyone else.

Binod Bhar said, 'Dhiren-babu, please list the accusations he faces.'

Dhiren Ghosh looked embarrassedly at Haricharan Mitra, who sat up.

'The charges against Kshid-da are levelled by our boys. I mean the swimmers, who have been representing the club in various competitions for seven or eight years, winning medals and making us proud.'

'Rubbish,' Kshitish said feelingly. 'They might be winning medals, but they've done nothing to make us proud. Shyamal used to do the 100-metre freestyle in a minute and four seconds four years ago; his timing is still the same. Does that make us proud?'

Haricharan continued as if he hadn't heard. 'These swimmers are the life-blood of the club. They are the reason why the club has survived, progressed. They are young and high-spirited. To handle them, one has to mingle with them as one of their own, understand them, keep pace with the times.'

'Does that mean they'll hang about idly for hours, skip their studies, neglect their training—does that constitute high spirits? I have to be "modern" to keep up with them—and only then I can handle them?'

'But Kshid-da, I'm sorry to say, doesn't have the ability to read their minds and temperaments.'

All eyes turned to Haricharan. Three or four heads nodded in support of what he had said. Behind his thick glasses, Kshitish blinked.

'In front of the juniors, Kshid-da taunted Shyamal by comparing his time with a 12-year-old American girl's. He threatened to throw out Gobindo, who went to the nationals in Bombay last year and currently holds the Bengal breaststroke record. Suhash was down with influenza and missed training for 10 days—Kshid-da went to his home and abused his parents. Amiya and Bela quit Jupiter and joined Apollo only because of Kshid-da; he wanted them to cut their hair short, and insisted they work out with barbells, like men. He cribbed about their dress and appearance every single day. Last year, as you know, those two girls won Apollo the team championship in the state meet.'

Haricharan paused. He hadn't glanced at Kshitish during his speech. Now he looked at him, and found him smiling mischievously. He turned around uncomfortably towards Dhiren Ghosh, Prafulla Basak and Bodu Chatterjee.

Rummaging in his pocket for snuff, Bodu Chatterjee cleared his throat and sat up straight.

'Mr. President, I have an observation to make. The coach should command the respect and faith of the boys and girls. They should be able to obey his suggestions blindly. But are they able to trust what Kshitish says?'

To create some drama, Bodu Chatterjee took a breather. He pulled out a handkerchief, blew his nose, returned the hanky to his pocket.

'Kshitish has never swum a single stroke. I've never known him to take part in a competition. Why should the boys and girls listen to him?'

'What's that!' President Binod Bhar looked at Kshitish in amazement. 'You don't know how to swim?'

Kshitish shook his head. 'When he says I can't swim, Bodu must mean I have never won a single competitive medal. Right?'

'Yes, yes, that's what I said!' Bodu said agitatedly. 'A coach needs to have a reputation. Otherwise, why would the kids obey him? Why do they listen to Haricharan? He was a national champion, he has even been to the

Olympics. He won the 13-mile Ganga competition three consecutive times.'

'You went to the Olympics?' Binod Bhar asked wonderingly.

'I represented India in the 1500-metre in the 1948 London Olympics,' Haricharan said slightly pompously. 'I was part of the water polo team as well.'

'What was the result?' the president leaned forward on the table.

Haricharan ran a rapid eye over everyone at the table, gulped and replied, 'I missed the bronze by point five seconds.'

Kshitish suddenly had a coughing fit. Everyone turned to look at him. After collecting himself, he apologized.

The visibly irritated president refocused his attention on Haricharan.

'McLane, an American, won the gold,' Haricharan said. 'Back at the poolside he told me that he'd been extra charged up by the competition I put up to him.'

'Really? What did you say?'

'What could I say, I congratulated him and told him that if I could have matched the timings I'd set back in India . . .' Haricharan stopped.

Someone was clearing his throat. The president said exasperatedly, 'You're coughing again? It must be a disease!'

Looking down, Kshitish mumbled, 'Hari, what would you have got—a gold or silver?'

Haricharan said agitatedly, 'I never said anything about a medal. Why are you insinuating things?'

'Jealousy!' observed Bodu, slapping his snuff box for emphasis.

'Kshitish just talks rubbish.' Kartik Saha finally joined in. 'I've seen it over and over again—he can't stand Hari.'

'Be it jealousy or whatever, Kshid-da, what pleasure do you get by making a laughing stock of me?'

Kshitish took off his spectacles and placed them on the table. 'What are the other charges against me, Dhiren?' he asked grimly.

Dhiren Ghosh hurriedly bent over his papers. 'Similar charges. All brought by the swimmers. They are waiting outside. If the president wants them to, they can come in here and tell us about them.'

'There's no need.' Kshitish put his glasses back on. 'All the charges are valid.'

The faces around the table brightened. Some nodded, a few sat up straight. Their gestures asked a single question: So, friend, where do you go from here?

'I know what they'll say. They'll say I don't join them in the pool; I tell them to work hard, abuse them if they don't do as I say. You'll say that I haven't yielded results for three or four years, that my attitude is prompting the swimmers to rebel.'

'He's even threatened to slap them.' No sooner had he uttered these words, Dhiren and Haricharan frowned at

Jogeshwar, who left the room in consternation, murmuring something about the delayed tea.

'Naturally, I will need to reply to the charges.'

The president said gravely, 'As you wish. If you have anything to say, of course we'll hear you out.'

The entire room waited anxiously. Kshitish took off his glasses and closed his eyes. 'I joined this club 35 years ago. Dhiren also came around the same time. Haricharan arrived five years later. I love Jupiter as much as they do. I, too, want glory for Jupiter—I want it to be the best club in the country. I want our swimmers, our water polo players, our divers, to win us glory. The more their performances improve, the more kudos they win for us. Whatever we try to do is for their betterment. That's why I've been hard, even abusive.'

Kshitish's sombre tone and manner had affected the entire room. 'The world has made unbelievable advances in swimming. But here each record is 10 or 15 years old. Sachin Nag's record is 25 years old. Why have we come to a halt? We have to progress in tandem with the world.'

'This is nothing new; we all know it,' Haricharan said self-importantly, glancing at the president. 'But where's the most essential ingredient—where's the diet? Where's the fuel for their hard work? Since we don't have the right food, what's the point in making them slog themselves into ill-health?'

'Exactly! Where's the diet?' Jogeshwar thumped the table hard.

The president and Dhiren Ghosh nodded. Jodu took a large pinch of snuff from his box.

'Nonsense,' Kshitish said in a quiet, determined voice. 'I've never heard of anyone fall ill after swimming. It's an excuse for a bunch of unambitious slackers. We don't train them hard enough to work off their diet. Shyamal and Gobindo—they got jobs not because of their education or intelligence, but because of their swimming skills. But what have they given back? They are ungrateful. If they spend even five rupees a day on food, lead a disciplined life, train hard, within a couple of years they can swim the 100-metre freestyle in a minute and the backstroke in a minute and a half.'

'Then why haven't you been able to train them?' asked Dhiren.

'If a student fails, the fault lies with the teacher,' Kartik nudged Bodu, who took up the refrain. 'Of course. You can't absolve yourself by labelling them ungrateful.'

'No, I am not absolving myself. Rather, I want to say that we shouldn't expect anything more of them. They're older now and jaded. There's no point in working on them.'

'I don't believe that.' Haricharan's shrillness startled Kshitish as well.

'You don't believe what?'

'Their times can be cut back further. I can do it. I can make them work. All this talk of jadedness is rubbish.'

Kshitish held Haricharan's stare for a few minutes.

'Then take the responsibility. I quit right now as chief trainer. My resignation letter will follow. I shan't come from tomorrow onwards.'

'How can you not come?' Bodu said hurriedly, 'You've been a member for so long!'

Kshitish smiled weakly, then his eyes gleamed. Addressing the president, he said, 'There's no rule that says one has to be a well-known swimmer to be a coach. None of the best-known coaches in the world—Talbot, Carlile, Gallagher, Haines, Counsilman—was an Olympic champion. They didn't need to jump into the pool to do their coaching. They train swimmers, not novices. One can observe swimmers much better from land, which is why I stay dry.'

'Kshid-da, I see you count yourself among these greats,' Jogeshwar said in feigned astonishment.

'They created world champions, Olympic champions—you haven't even managed a Bengal champion!' The mockery was evident in Kartik Saha's voice.

'He can, of course he can. We'll set a world record soon, won't we, Kshitish?' Dhiren Ghosh smiled slyly.

'It's not possible to craft a champion swimmer in this country,' president Binod Bhar finally had his say.

Kshitish stood up. 'That's not possible anywhere in the world,' he said tiredly, walking towards the door. 'Champions are born, not made. We have to look out for them, identify their potential.'

'That's right, Kshid-da, now go on a penance for them.'

'Kshitish, have your tea at least.'

'Kshitish-babu, you must continue to come to the club regularly.'

As soon as he left the room, Kshitish ran into Shyamal, Gobindo and four or five others. He looked each one in the eye. They stiffened.

'I've scolded you a lot, abused you even. No longer. I have quit as a trainer with this club. Keep swimming with passion.'

Kshitish walked out slowly from the club.

The dark waters of Kamaldighi reflected the park lights as elongated chalk-marks. The clock atop the Jupiter clubhouse read five minutes to eight. The pool was circular in shape, edged with a brick path now teeming with people. Card games such as Auction Bridge and Twenty-nine were in progress under the lights. Occasional whoops rose from the card-playing groups. The benches were packed. Flowering shrubs were enclosed behind iron railings. Groups of gossiping young men were clustered around them. Streetfood sellers were doing roaring business.

Kshitish stood gripping the railings, staring into the darkened waters. The Apollo clubhouse was bang opposite Jupiter. The concrete pillars of the diving board rose up in the darkness like giant limbs from the water.

'Kshid-da!'

A surprised Kshitish turned his head.

'Bhelo!'

'What happened, Kshid-da?'

'Nothing much. I quit.'

'Just as well. I hope there were no fights or scenes?'

'Nope.'

Kshitish turned to face the tank. The breeze was skimming the surface of the water, bearing droplets of water and the smell of weeds and fish. Kshitish had inhaled this aroma for 35 years. For him, there was no superior fragrance in the world.

Bhelo came to stand by him.

'Bhelo, tell me what you think I should do now. I'm totally unemployed.'

'Maybe you could look after Prajapati. Boudi is a lady, after all; her assistants are also female. A business requires a man. There's no saying when there'll be need of you!'

'Your Boudi looks tiny, but she beats me hollow when it comes to work. I can't be much more than a watchman at Prajapati.'

'Then?'

Kshitish returned his gaze to the water.

'Kshid-da, if you promise not to get angry, can I say something?'

Kshitish looked at him.

'Go to Apollo.'

'No, they are Jupiter's rivals. A handful of selfish, greedy ignoramuses gangs up against me and throws me out, but does that mean I join hands with the enemies?'

'But there you will get the facilities, you'll get young swimmers to train; you want work, you'll get work. You have to avenge your humiliation. What's the point in discriminating between friends and enemies?'

A troubled Kshitish kept silent. The debate that consumed him prohibited any fair decisions at the moment. He felt a kinship with Jupiter, but his only aim in life was to train swimmers. If he had to fulfil his ambition, he would have to turn his back on his own. But could he do that? Kshitish shook his head.

'Then consider joining another club.'

'I won't be able to stick around anywhere for long.' Kshitish began walking fast.

'So you'll just sit at home?' Bhelo hitched up his trousers, almost running to keep pace with Kshitish.

'I want to do some real work. Something that will prove a point to everyone. I'll create a champion. I'll build her in my own image. If I could just find someone–anyone.'

Kshitish walked out rapidly through the gates and merged with the crowds on the street. Bhelo stared after him for a while, then told the alukaabliwallah, 'Make me four annas worth, extra spicy.'

{4}

It was nearly eight in the morning. Kshitish had come back from the market. He no longer went to Jupiter. Through the day he had no work at all. Shopping, in fact, was primary among his daily duties. Every day, he took the narrow alleyways through the nearby slum to the market and came back the other way, via Central Avenue, past the Children's Park.

On the way back today, he had seen that the park was very crowded. Tables and chairs were laid out under a shed. Hindi film songs were playing over the loudspeaker. An announcement cut into them abruptly: 'Organized by the Netaji Balak Sangha, a 20-hour nonstop walking contest. The competition began at eight o'clock last evening and will end at four o'clock today.'

After a muffled altercation over the kind of language that should be used for the announcements, another voice took over the microphone: 'The competition began last evening at eight p.m., after the inauguration by yesteryear footballer Mr. Krishnaprasad Maiti. The competition will close this afternoon at four. The prizes will be distributed by the respected leader, our organization's chief patron, Mr. Bishtucharan Dhar. Twenty-two contestants had entered the competition, eight have dropped out.'

Kshitish's gaze suddenly fell on a dark figure, tall and thin as a bamboo reed.

The circular park was surrounded by a railing. About three yards inside the railing, a cement path encircled a grassy patch. The contestants were walking slowly and tiredly around the trail. Most of them were 16 or 17 years old. They would have to continue walking through the afternoon, the cement beneath their feet almost as hot as the midsummer sun beating down on them. Each circuit was about 75 metres long.

She was dressed in ill-fitting trousers, a loose shirt, ordinary slippers. Her hair, though cropped short like a boy's at the front, nearly touched her shoulders. Kshitish left the road for a spot at the railing.

His eyes began to follow only this one contestant. Children and youngsters made up most of the crowd inside the park. Older people just about spared a glance for them as they went about their business outside on the road. Sleeplessness, tiredness and hunger were evident on the contestants' faces. One or two exchanged a few tired smiles or a couple of words with familiar people. The three boys whom Kshitish had seen with the girl on the Ganga, were walking beside her on the grass, talking to her. Koni tried to shoo them off. Then she slipped off her footwear, extracted from her pocket the lozenges she'd been given by the organizers, gave them one each and popped one into her own mouth. Continuing to walk, she gestured for water and a member of the Netaji Balak Sangha came running with a glass. After three or four rounds, she put on her slippers again.

Kshitish was jolted back to reality when his neighbour, Amulya-babu, stopped on his way to office to ask him, 'What are you watching, Kshitish-babu, the sporting Bengali?'

Kshitish didn't care for the man at all, or for his dramatic sarcasm.

'What can they do—after all, we haven't really done anything to encourage sports. So they do the best they can.'

Ending the conversation, Kshitish set off home. The front door was locked. Lilabati was out. Kshitish did have a key, though. Glancing at the clock, he did a double-take: he was almost 50 minutes late. Which meant Lilabati must have been so angry that she had left without cooking.

Kshitish started preparations for the meal. As he chopped the vegetables, all he wanted to do was go back to the park and watch Koni. This was the second time he had seen her.

Kshitish didn't care at all for this nonstop walking thing. It didn't require any brains, only brawn. It didn't call for speed, strong muscles or competitiveness. He objected vehemently to calling it a sport at all.

He had once made his feelings very clear at Goldighi, where a swimmer had set out to create a world record by swimming 90 hours without a break. 'You fool, when we've never won even an Olympic medal in swimming, you want to do the country proud with these gimmicks?' he had screamed.

If four or five acquaintances hadn't held Kshitish back, he would have probably plunged into the water and messed up the potential world record. He did acknowledge, though, that these nonstop events helped identify people with endurance as well as stubbornness. But what was the point if they weren't cultivated for a higher end through disciplined training and technique!

What a waste. It troubled Kshitish, troubled him very much. For the moment though, he was impatient to return to the park. He got up to check the time, and calculated that Koni had been walking for nearly 14 hours. Six crucial hours to go. Would she survive?

* * *

Kshitish placed the cooker on the stove, locked the door and set out again.

The crowd of spectators had thinned at the park. A few people lingered under trees while the organizers sat in the shed. Koni was walking, a torn straw hat on her head. Kshitish counted: thirteen remained. One person had opted out. He entered the park and made his way to the shade of a tree. When Koni passed by, he observed her keenly. Droplets of sweat were running down her cheeks to her chin. Her eyes were sunken, high cheekbones even more prominent, lips dry. But something about the way she carried herself, straight and tall, told Kshitish that she wouldn't stop even if it rained fire.

Why exactly he felt this way, Kshitish couldn't have said. He only knew that you could tell a lot about what a man thinks of himself by the way he holds his head when he walks.

Kshitish returned home at noon. Lilabati was talking to two girls from the shop. Kshitish asked her, 'What happened to the room in Hatibagan?'

'They want a huge advance. It won't work.'

He went indoors, absent-mindedly followed his bath-lunch routine, all the while with an eye on the clock. As soon as it struck three, he set out again.

From thirteen, the number had dropped to eight—five more people had opted out. The park was quite crowded now. The loudspeaker was being used for announcements, not songs, one of them informing the contestants that they had just 50 minutes to go.

Koni was still walking, as Kshitish had known she would be. Exhaustion dogged her footsteps. The three boys from the morning were still with her, walking on the edge of the grass. She laughed a couple of times at something they said. Kshitish noticed she was dragging her right leg. Among the other contestants were two 10-year-olds, who still looked quite fresh.

'Our chief guest, beloved leader of the public and our wellwisher, Mr Bishtucharan Dhar, is here today despite immense pressure on his time. We are proud to have him amongst us.'

After hearing the announcement, Kshitish trained his sights on the shed. A white tablecloth and two flower vases had appeared in the meantime. Seated behind them was the chief guest for the day.

It was the hippo from the ghats! Kshitish was taken aback.

'Twenty minutes to go before the competition ends. Prizes will be distributed immediately afterwards.'

A few muffled sounds were heard over the loudspeaker. 'We forgot to mention that the chief guest will deliver a speech ahead of distributing the prizes.'

All eight finished the course. Nearly 100 people of all ages had gathered around the shed. Kshitish joined them, his eyes searching for Koni. He found her seated on the cement steps, her legs splayed, her hands massaging her right thigh.

'No way am I signing up again for a walking race. There isn't even any ranking!'

'I told you so many times, don't bother. Bhadu and I took part once and realised right away it was all rubbish.'

'But Kanti said people actually come and pin money on you!'

'Not in these minor competitions.'

'Says who! If Koni had been in a frock, she'd have got at

least 20 or 25 rupees. She looks like a boy in shirt and trousers.'

'No way–people here are just stingy.'

'No, Bhadu is quite right,' Koni said, 'I do look like a boy in these clothes. Chandu, just check what the prizes are. I've been out the whole day–Ma will kill me if I go back empty-handed.'

The formal announcements had ended. Chief guest Bishtu Dhar had started on his speech.

Kshitish was standing a short distance away from Koni, listening to their conversation. Now he came forward and asked her, 'Do you want to learn how to swim?'

Koni raised her face, stared in irritation into the bright eyes behind the thick lenses, topped by salt-and-pepper hair. Then she returned to massaging her leg.

'Do you want to learn swimming?'

'I can swim.'

'No, you can't.'

Koni jerked her head up. 'What do you know?'

'I've seen you in the Ganga. Not that kind of swimming. Swimming has to be learnt.'

'What I know takes me across the Ganga and back. Why do I need to know anything more?'

'There's a lot more to learn.'

'I don't need to learn anything more; what I know is enough.' Ignoring Kshitish, Koni stood up and shouted, 'Gopal, come here a minute.'

Tearing his eyes away from the pile of prizes on the table, a 12-year-old boy in a torn vest and bare feet came up to Koni.

'Did Ma say anything?'

'Just wait till you get home—she'll skin you alive.'

'Dada?'

'Dada hasn't gone to work today, he's ill. He fought with Ma for you. He said you did the right thing.'

Kshitish decided to approach Koni one more time. But by then the organizers had whisked her away. Each participant was being given a packet of food.

'The body has to be trained to be your slave.'

Kshitish turned to look at the speaker—a lump of fat in white behind the microphone. Kshitish negotiated the crowd to advance towards the shed.

'But how will you do it? You may have lakhs and lakhs of rupees, but can you arch your body, can you hold the peacock pose? If someone cuffs you and runs away, would you be able to give chase? No, you couldn't, I know you couldn't.'

A voice piped up from behind the chief guest: 'Should I give it a shot?'

Bishtu Dhar turned back, saw Kshitish and frowned. Covering the microphone, he growled, 'Don't make a joke of everything.' He removed his hands from the microphone and began again, 'Do you know why you can't? It's because you are not fit. Fitness comes from regular exercise.'

Bishtu Dhar looked at Kshitish, who nodded approvingly.

'That is why we all need to work out. Walking, too, is an exercise. That is why I told the young officials of the Netaji Balak Sangha, who have made such a success of today's contest, "organize the walk, I'll be there by your side. This is social work, I will walk beside you".'

'Nope, not by their side, but showing the way. Leaders have to be in the forefront.'

Bishtu Dhar looked back and frowned. Then he nodded. 'But why should I be by your side? I will be leading the way. Whenever people get together to do something for society, to make people healthier, I will come running before the rest.'

'Ease up on the running bit,' came the whisper. 'What if someone asks for a demo?'

Bishtu Dhar gulped. 'But why should I come running! When does a man run? When he is scared, directionless. But if the people are with me, why should I run? The people will tell us which way to go, so why should we seek direction? No, I shall not be scared if you are with me. I shall be guided by you in serving you and the country. That is why I end by addressing the contestants: If you aren't fit, you can't work. And if you can't work, you can't build a country. With this competition, your walk begins today . . .' Bishtu Dhar groped in his pockets. 'This walk . . . this walk of life . . .' he said, before looking back helplessly.

'You've forgotten the speech?'

Nodding haplessly, Bishtu Dhar said, 'I had a Tagore poem to quote, can't find it now.'

'Say "this journey, which begins in this tiny park—"'

The microphone boomed again with the chief guest's emotion-laden voice. 'This journey, which begins in this tiny park—'

'May it gradually guide you to a larger life of happiness and prosperity. May this circumambulation of the park evolve into a circumambulation of the world. Jai Hind!'

Bishtu Dhar echoed Kshitish word for word, only adding a trembling 'Inquilaab Zindabad' after the 'Jai Hind'.

The prizes were given away. All those who had stuck out the 20 hours received a plastic kit bag and a towel. Those who quit after 16 hours got a bag each, while the ones who had retired after 12 hours got just the towel. After receiving her prize, Koni examined her bag, but didn't feel the need to thank the chief guest. Tucking the food packet into the bag, she handed it over to her brother, saying, 'Let's go home, we have to give this to Ma.'

Koni placed her hand on her brother's shoulder and walked away, limping.

Kshitish stared after her. Her head was held high, her body swaying like a bamboo reed. Bhadu and Chandu were with her. Out of the park, they slowly disappeared from sight. It occurred to Kshitish that he should have taken down her address.

'Beshtada's asking for you.'

'Beshtada who?' Kshitish asked absently.

'Our chief guest today.'

Bishtu Dhar smiled widely on seeing Kshitish, saying, 'Everyone's saying the ending was fabulous.' Then he whispered, 'There's a reason I tagged on the Inquilaab Zindabad bit. I needed to emphasise my progressiveness. Come with me, I have a car, I'll explain everything on the way.'

Bishtu Dhar planned to fight the next general elections, for which he had already begun the groundwork. He was putting up money for various local events and delivering speeches as chief guest. He would contest the elections as an independent social worker.

As the car drew up at his door, Bishtu Dhar told Kshitish, 'I need you.'

'Me?'

'Yes, I need you to be my speech-writer. I'll pay you, of course. All right?'

'But I don't know anything besides sports!' Kshitish tried to absorb the shock.

'That's precisely why I need you. My speeches will be on sports, not on any other subject. Binod Bhar, the current MLA, has a sporting background. He's president of several clubs. I, too, will run my campaign on the same lines. Binod Bhar wants to be a minister.'

Biting into a singara, Kshitish said, 'Let me think it over.'

{5}

A one-mile swimming contest had been organized at Rabindra Sarovar. Twenty-five people were taking part—twenty-two boys and three girls.

There was a crush at the starting point. The contestants were busy oiling themselves. At the request of the Dhakuria Sporting Club, the organizers, Kshitish had agreed to play referee, using a boat to keep up with the swimmers.

Afloat in the boat just ahead of the starting point, Bhelo asked Kshitish, 'Kshid-da, who do you think will win? I think it will be Subir.'

'I think it's wrong of Subir to compete. He's a junior national record-holder—he shouldn't be taking part in such contests.'

'I agree. The rest seem fairly raw.'

Scrutinizing the line-up of swimmers, Bhelo asked, 'Who's the girl in red? Don't think I've ever seen her before.'

Disadvantaged by the distance and his thick glasses,

Kshitish could only see a fair body in a red costume, topped by a white cap.

'How would I know who she is!'

'I was just wondering . . . I saw the Ballygunge Club coach, Pranabendu Biswas, with her. She seems to be well-off—I saw her get off that green car there. I think her parents are with her.'

'You notice too much.'

'How can I not notice her—she's like a wax doll! Just look at the girl next to her—like a lump of black clay! How funny they look together.'

Kshitish peered closely at the figures. A few moments later, he breathed one word: 'Koni!'

Precisely at that moment, the starter's pistol came to life with a bang.

Having allowed the swimmers a lead, Kshitish's boat began following them.

Subir and about 10 others were clustered together right in front. Immediately behind was another big bunch. Bringing up the rear were the three girls and two young boys.

For about 500 metres, the last five kept pace with one another. Then the red costumed-girl began pulling away.

'Kshid-da, do you see that stroke! How she keeps afloat . . .'

Kshitish observed her for a while. 'She isn't moving her head properly. If she doesn't position it dead-centre, it will impact her balance, slow her down. And her body is rolling more than it should. Her elbows should rise higher . . .'

'There you go, finding faults.'

'But how will she improve if I don't find faults?'

'She isn't your student, is she?'

'So what?'

Now a few of the swimmers in the first two groups were losing momentum. Kshitish looked back. Koni was advancing with the two youngest boys, using her arms like paddles, moving her head from side to side. About 20 metres ahead was a solitary girl, swimming steadily. The red-costumed girl was 30 metres in front, about 10 arm-lengths behind one of the boys.

'Koee-neeeeeeee.'

The cry came drifting from the eastern bank of the lake.

Kshitish and Bhelo turned around together to see a dark, sickly young man, about 25 years of age, racing along the bank. He was dressed in a dhoti and a blue shirt, and clutching his slippers in his hands.

'Koee-neeeeeeee . . . . Koee-neeeeeeeee.'

The voice was now sounding like a wail. Spectators had gathered on the bank; the young man could be glimpsed running through the crowd, pausing occasionally. Helplessness was writ large on his face.

'Koee-neeeeeeee.'

The wail trailed off despairingly. Kshitish looked around

to see the two kids moving ahead, leaving Koni behind. Red Costume had beaten the two boys.

'Who's he, Kshid-da?'

'I don't know, must be some contestant's relative.'

A green Fiat was crawling along the bank, honking frequently, anxiety evident in the two male and female faces at the windows.

'Koee-neeeeeeee.'

The boat continued to glide across the water. The young man in blue was now resting against a tree trunk. Gradually, he became smaller and smaller in Kshitish's view. Way behind, two arms continued to rise and fall in the water. Then they fell out of sight altogether, the setting sun glistening periodically on the disturbed water.

A commotion rose ahead. The first competitor had crossed the finishing line. Probably Subir.

By the time Koni completed the course, a number of contestants were ready to go home. Someone was reading out the Dhakuria Sporting Club's annual achievements into the microphone in a monotone. No one noticed the last contestant cross the finishing line.

The banks of the lake were muddy. Koni was up to her calves in mud, her body bent forward, when she suddenly came to a halt and looked up. Her eyes were bloodshot. Her cheap black costume stuck to her body as she panted, the ribs in her back shaking spasmodically. Her shoulder bones were sticking out, her long, skinny arms hung by her side. A short distance away, the blue-shirted young man pretended he was listening to the voice coming over the loudspeaker.

Koni emerged, shaking. Two boys about her own age conversed between themselves, perhaps a tad too loudly.

'At least she finished the course.'

'A bit slower and she'd have topped the competition next year.'

Koni looked up at the young man. His face wore the shame and humiliation of someone who had just been slapped.

'Do you want to learn how to swim?'

A startled Koni turned back.

The same man. Salt-and-pepper hair, crew cut. Thick glasses.

'The red-costumed girl knew how to swim, that's how she defeated you. You can beat her if you learn.'

Abruptly, Koni's eyes filled with tears. Her lips trembled. Then, almost immediately, her jaw became firm.

Only Bhelo noticed the way Kshitish's eyes lit up. Bhelo shook his head uncomfortably.

'Who's that over there?'

'My brother.'

Koni dragged herself towards the dressing room. Kshitish advanced towards Koni's brother.

'I am a swimming coach. My name is Kshitish Sinha. I want to train your sister.' Kshitish went straight to the point.

'I am Kamal Pal. I used to swim at Apollo at one time. I've seen you from a distance.' Kamal tried to bring some life into his yellowish, sickly eyes. Then he shook his head. 'We're very poor. We don't have the money for swimming lessons.'

'I don't want to be paid.'

'It's not that. Swimming calls for other expenses, on food, for instance. That's why I couldn't do it—because we didn't have enough to eat. My father used to work in a packaging factory, he died of TB. After my swimming training, I used to writhe with hunger. I used to drop off to sleep in school. Then, after my father died, I quit school, quit swimming. That was five years ago.'

'What do you do for a living? How big is your family?'

'There used to be seven of us siblings and our mother. I'm the eldest. One of my brothers was electrocuted on the railway lines last year. The third lives in Kanchrapara, with an aunt. Then come Koni, two sisters and another brother. I'm employed in a garage in Rajabazar, earning 150 rupees a month after working overtime. That's what we live on. We live in a slum in Shyampukur.'

Kamal became breathless. He seemed to be suppressing his excitement. He had revealed everything about his family's financial condition without any shame or hesitation. Kshitish, however, felt anxious about the way he was losing his breath. He remembered Kamal's father had died of TB.

'I wanted to be a famous swimmer. Koni, too, has been keen on sports since her childhood. I wanted her to take up a sport. I've heard she swims in the Ganga, though I've never seen her. I've heard she hangs about with boys all day. A lot of people tell me a lot of things. Actually, I only get back home to sleep. I don't know what anybody is up to. Still, I spank her sometimes if I lose my temper. I can't do much more. Even if I want to, I don't have the means to sponsor her swimming lessons.'

'That's my responsibility.'

'What do you mean?' Bhelo finally spoke up. 'What do you mean it's your responsibility?'

'It means exactly what it sounds like,' Kshitish answered irritatedly, and then turned to Kamal. 'If the family doesn't help, the coaching will be useless. I just want you to cooperate. The rest is my responsibility.'

'If you take the responsibility, that's my good fortune.' Kamal's eyes suddenly shone through the pallor. 'But I can't spend even a paisa. I borrowed 12 rupees yesterday to buy her a costume. It's poor-quality stuff. I'd never seen her swim; this was the first time. She'd promised to come first among the girls—you saw what happened.'

Kshitish nodded.

Bhelo said, 'She has no strength, she could barely pull herself ahead after the halfway mark. We have to feed her well. Isn't that so, Kshid-da?'

'We should go now.'

Kshitish turned around to see Koni standing far away. She was wearing a frock, a bag slung over her shoulder.

'I really want her to learn how to swim, to become famous.' Kamal hesitated, then added, 'And whatever I can scrimp and save, I'll spend on her training.'

Meanwhile, the prizes were being distributed. The names and applause came floating over the loudspeaker.

'First among girls . . .'

Kshitish looked towards the siblings. They were walking away empty-handed, aiming to squeeze through a gap in the railings to reach the road. Kamal slipped through. About to follow him, Koni held back for a moment.

'. . . is Hiya Mitra of Ballygunge Swimming Club. Time: 35 minutes, 18 seconds.'

Koni bent and passed through the gap.

'Have you lost your mind, Kshid-da?'

'Why do you say that?'

'That thin, dark girl, with no money for food or clothes—you'll teach her how to swim, and you'll take responsibility for her as well?'

'Yes. Is there any other way to teach someone?'

'What sort of responsibility will you take for her?'

'Of feeding and clothing her, building up her mental strength, which is the most important thing. Coaching her regularly. All of it.'

'Then you'd have to bring her home.'

'If it comes to that, I'll have to. Once upon a time disciples did live in their gurus' homes. That was a good way of doing it.'

'You've considered Boudi, right?'

Kshitish was about to reply angrily when he held back, focusing his attention towards the loudspeaker.

'Kanakchampa Pal, unattached contestant. Kanakchampa Pal.' Then they heard the whispered words, 'She's probably left. Let it be.'

Kshitish saw a shy-faced Hiya standing next to the green Fiat. Her delight was evident in her dimples. A lady was holding the medal in her hands and smiling. Pranabendu was standing with them. Trying to explain something to a handsome, well-dressed gentleman, he moved his arms in the butterfly stroke.

'We'll see you next year,' Kshitish spoke to himself.

'Did you say something, Kshid-da?'

Kshitish didn't reply.

'You're going to coach her, but where's the pool?' Bhelo said. 'You are no longer a trainer with Jupiter. So where will you go? You have to consider another club.'

'No, I'll coach her at Jupiter itself. Let's see who stops me. But before that I have to ensure an income, Bhelo. I need money. I must go and meet Bishtu Dhar.'

{6}

They were in the middle of lunch and visibly surprised when Kshitish suddenly appeared at their door. 'I have to talk to you, could you come out for a minute?'

Having addressed Koni, Kshitish stepped away from the door. In that brief time, he had taken in all there was to see: A couple of green chillies, some onions, rice starch with possibly some grains of rice, and a bit of tamarind. Five people with alloy and aluminium plates. A wooden cot, no mattresses, a few oil-stained pillows. A few shirts and trousers hung on a string stretched across the wall. The thatched room had just the one window, overlooking a sewage-filled drain.

Koni came out, her eyes curious.

'Sign this form. You'll be coming with me to Jupiter this afternoon.'

Koni took the form, but didn't quite seem to know what to do with it. 'Do you have a pen?'

Kshitish wasn't carrying one.

'Can I use a pencil?'

'No, you need a pen.'

Koni disappeared for a moment and came back with a pen. Her hand hovering over the space Kshitish had indicated, she asked, 'In English or Bengali?'

'Whatever you want.'

Koni laboriously signed the form in English, muttering under her breath all the while. Watching the effort, Kshitish asked, 'Which class?'

'Class five.'

'Do you go to school?'

'They threw me out.'

'Wait for me at the western entrance to Kamaldighi at exactly four o'clock. Carry your towel and costume.'

'I don't have a towel.'

'Okay, I'll bring one. Be there on time.'

* * *

Koni was there right on time. Kshitish escorted her into the club. Haricharan and Prafulla Basak were in the office. Kshitish handed over the form to Prafulla, who asked, 'Swimmer?'

'Yes.'

'She'll have to take a trial.'

'What do you mean?' Kshitish asked belligerently. 'Isn't it enough that I'm vouching for her?'

'It doesn't work like that—every club has its rules,' said Prafulla, glancing at Haricharan, who was smirking to himself while gazing out of the window. 'Only a trainer can certify someone as a swimmer. Otherwise, just about anybody would be bringing in people from the streets and claiming they're swimmers—and if they drown, we'd be in a soup.'

'Anybody! Am I anybody?' Kshitish voice was low, menacing. Koni, meanwhile, was totally entranced by the groups of boys clad in trunks, emerging from the club. There were a few girls as well. Outside, in the pool, the 'novice' swimmers were creating a ruckus.

'Okay, put her through a trial.'

Haricharan finally looked their way. Sizing up Koni, he asked, 'Who is she?'

'I know the girl. She has potential. We have to teach her the strokes, though.'

'Has potential!' Haricharan spat out the words. 'If she has to be taught the strokes, she will be coached by a club trainer. Let her come tomorrow morning. Bandana or Tunu will put her through her paces.'

Kshitish looked hard at Prafulla and Haricharan. A few seconds passed before he said, 'Okay.'

'What happened—they didn't admit me?' Koni asked the moment they left the office.

'You have to appear for a test. Not just you, Koni, both of us will be tested.'

Koni didn't quite get it. 'Both of us? Both of us will be tested? Why, don't you know how to swim?'

'Not swimming. They'll test my tolerance for insult.'

Kshitish headed towards the railings skirting the tank. Nearly 400 members of either club, including some girls, were splashing about in the water. A few boys were perched on the diving boards, occasionally performing lazy dives. Kshitish shook his head disconsolately. No-one was putting in any real effort.

Stepping into the pool, Suhash looked at Kshitish and immediately looked away.

'Two 400's, then a 100 each of butterfly, backstroke and breaststroke—you remember, right?' Haricharan called out through the office window. Suhash nodded.

Kshitish grimaced. Barely 1,100 metres—did they expect to make progress with such sparse training? Still, Suhash's strokes were flawless. Kshitish said, 'Koni, watch that fellow—note how he uses his arms.'

Koni observed Suhash. At one point, Kshitish said, 'His arms are dipping into the water just ahead of his head, going in and coming out again near his thighs. Quick arm-strokes are most important—so that random way you swim in the river won't wash. The arm movements have to be clean, firm. The actual pace is powered by the muscles of the shoulders, back and arms—which is why you have to exercise. See how he holds his head? Does he move it around, like you do? His face is in the water, see, he's turning it to the side just to inhale. The more you move your head, the more speed you lose. And his shoulders, see, they jut out of the water.'

It wasn't clear if Koni, staring fixedly at the swimmers, was taking in any of this. Suddenly, she asked, 'That girl there, what's her name?'

Kshitish felt let down. 'I don't know,' he replied.

'The costume she's wearing—what is it made of?'

'Nylon. It's very expensive.'

'It's beautiful.'

Kshitish thought for a moment. 'I'll buy you one—'

Koni turned around to face him, her eyes shining.

'. . . the day you can swim like that,' Kshitish pointed at Suhash.

Koni looked back at Suhash with keen eyes, then grimaced contemptuously, 'I can learn that in two days.'

'Good. Wait for me at the same spot at six-thirty tomorrow morning. Bring your costume. You'll pass the test; I'm not worried about that. But if either Panna or Nirmal is asked to teach you the strokes, we've had it.'

* * *

Koni passed, but they still didn't take her in.

Kshitish was present during the trials in the morning. Koni aced the 200 metres, trod water with her arms in the air, dove into the pool from the lower rung of the diving board.

In the evening, Prafulla told Kshitish, 'Not possible, we can't take in more members. Strict orders from the secretary. There's not an inch of space in the pool, it's so crowded. We had to turn back two people today.'

'Why didn't you tell me earlier?' Kshitish was about to explode, but checked himself.

'It skipped my mind.'

Shooting out of the club like a bullet from a gun, the first person Kshitish spotted was Haricharan, talking to two boys at the starting platform.

'Haricharan!' Kshitish screamed. 'You wanted to be the chief trainer—now you are. What are these games you're still playing!'

Haricharan looked around irritatedly. 'What games?'

'Why wasn't my girl accepted?'

'Go and ask Prafulla.'

'Oh, I've already heard his flimsy excuses. Mark my words—one day, that girl will disgrace you. You'll regret it then!'

'Ah, right, that girl you brought in yesterday. So let her. At least Bengal will be getting a woman swimmer, right!'

'Not Bengal—India!' Gripping the railing as he shook, Kshitish shouted hoarsely, 'You can't create swimmers on the foundation of Olympic lies—you'll be caught out one day.'

Prafulla came out of the office room.

'What's all this ranting, Kshid-da?'

'Stop me if you can! You don't own the ground I'm standing on! How low can you stoop! You refused to accept the girl; you think there's no other club in the world? You think Jupiter's the only one?"

'Then go to some other club!' Haricharan shouted back. 'There, there's one right alongside.'

'I will too, I will!'

Kshitish strode rapidly towards Apollo. Behind him, Prafulla addressed the crowd of curious onlookers, 'Mad, he's mad.'

* * *

Near the Apollo gate, Kshitish came to with a start. What am I doing here? These people are Jupiter's sworn enemies! Am I going to be a traitor?

However, he had already been spotted by Apollo's vice-president, Nakul Mukherjee. Coming down the stairs to the gate, he said, 'Kshitish, what's up? How come you're here?'

Kshitish suddenly heard himself saying, 'Would you have a place here, Nakul-da? Jupiter's thrown me out.'

'What are you saying! How can anyone throw you out!'

'Honest, Nakul-da, they've shown me the door. I'm not asking for money. I've come across a girl, I just need an opportunity to coach her.'

'Come in, tell me the whole story.'

'But before that, I have to tell you, I'm a Jupiter man; Apollo will never be my club.'

'Then why should we take you?'

'Don't take me, take the girl! I'll coach her. If she wins anything, it will be for Apollo.'

'Okay, okay, come inside now.'

'First tell me if you accept my terms. Apollo will go by what you say. So I'll come in only if you agree.'

Nakul Mukherjee looked intently at Kshitish for a few minutes. Then he said, 'Your departure from Jupiter will be like creating a chink in their armour. It's a victory for us if you come to Apollo. Okay, I accept your conditions.'

Before entering the club, Kshitish looked back one last time. The shadows were lengthening over Kamaldighi. The hands of the giant clock at Jupiter were indistinct to his bespectacled eyes. Kshitish felt a sudden, deep pang in his heart. His eyes glistened.

* * *

Sleep eluded Kshitish that night; he spent the time sitting up against the walls of the verandah. Just one worry swirled in his mind: 'Was I right? Should I have gone to Apollo?'

An excited Bhelo made an appearance bright and early the next morning.

'Kshid-da, you've joined Apollo? Excellent move! I told you long ago, this is war. And all's fair in war—there are no permanent friends or enemies.'

Kshitish was silent.

'We have to fix Jupiter now. Kshid-da, you need to forget all that heartstrings business . . .'

'Bhelo!'

Kshitish had raised one hand, his jaw determined, his eyes burning beneath the thick lenses. Bhelo retreated.

'Say one more word and I'll . . .'

'I'm sorry, forgive me, Kshid-da,' muttered Bhelo.

{7}

'No, no, no, how many times do I need to tell you that the elbow mustn't bend so much—why did the arm jump up like a paddle? No, that isn't working—the left shoulder is moving ahead with the left arm, leaving the right shoulder behind—so what happens to the square shoulder position? Come on, do it again. Hey now, what's that! When you pull your arm out of the water, your body's doing this whole crooked caterpillar walk! Try and grasp why your elbow isn't bending the way it should . . . yes, like that. Don't splay your fingers as you make the pull-back movement. No, don't slap the water so clumsily, your hands must go in cleanly. First the fingers, then the wrist, then the full arm. And understand the breathing technique. If you breathe when your head is turned to the right, then it should coincide with your left wrist entering the water. Keep your head down, chin to the chest. Your head must remain centred . . . Go on, do it again. Two weeks gone, and you still haven't managed to do one thing right.'

Standing on the narrow cemented ledge bordering the pool, Kshitish continued to issue instructions. Koni swam in the shallows, stopping intermittently to listen to him. The lesson had begun at six-thirty in the morning. It was eight-thirty now.

'No more, Kshid-da.'

'Why! You'd said you'd be swimming like Suhash in two days. It's been 17 days now.'

Treading water, Koni gritted her teeth. 'I am. But you keep saying I'm not.'

'If it isn't working out right, should I say it is?'

'It is working.'

'No, it isn't. Go over it again.'

'I don't feel like it.'

Koni advanced towards the ledge. Kshitish was momentarily lost for words, then he said, 'Learn your strokes and I'll buy you a nylon costume.'

'I don't want one.'

Koni heaved herself out of the pool. Kshitish knew that arm-twisting wouldn't work with her—she needed a bait to enthuse her.

'Hey, why are you leaving the pool? Hungry?'

Koni walked away silently towards the gate.

'You must be hungry. I'm thinking we should organize two eggs, two bananas and two slices of toast.'

Koni came to a stop. Kshitish calculated mentally—the tab would come to nearly a rupee.

'Starting today?'

Kshitish nodded. Koni paused, thinking, and then said, 'But I'll take the food home.'

Kshitish asked curiously, 'But why?'

'Just like that. I will not eat elsewhere.'

'Then you have to spend another half-an-hour in the pool.'

It broke Kshitish's heart to say those words. It was inhuman to dangle a carrot to make a starving Koni work harder. But he told himself that if one didn't push oneself beyond one's limitations, one would never overcome them. Let her work hard, even harder. Her body would reel in pain, would stagger, want to collapse before reaching the threshold of tolerance. And then she would have to challenge that threshold. To get there, she needed a strong character and stubborn determination.

'Go on, what are you hanging around for? Two eggs, two bananas, two slices of buttered toast.

'Get a grip on pain, Koni. If you don't get to know it, learn it or conquer it, how will you use it as a stepping stone to greater things? Right, you're doing good, the elbow not so high . . . face in the water. Pain and time are your opponents. And those two can't be separated. Even if you can defeat pain, you can't defeat time. Subdue time, and you can subdue pain.'

Leaning back against the railing, Kshitish continued to talk silently to Koni. Sometimes he shouted aloud. Only Koni was in the pool now. Three or four outsiders were taking a dip in the bathing ghat, and at the centre, a woman was washing utensils. The Jupiter and Apollo starting platforms, about 50 metres apart, were deserted, apart from four or five kids taking running jumps from the Jupiter springboard. A couple of men wolfing down telebhaja on the Jupiter verandah were laughing openly at Kshitish.

Amiya and Bela emerged from the interiors of Apollo, and paused to watch Koni in the pool. Amiya had returned to the pool today after a week; she had been busy with her college exams. Bela apparently didn't enjoy training without Amiya. Today they had both swum half a mile.

'Who's that girl?' asked Amiya.

'Kshid-da's discovery,' Bela rolled her eyes. 'Don't you remember what Haricharan-da said the other day? Kshid-da's apparently vowed to use that girl to teach Jupiter a lesson.'

'Are you serious? That girl can barely move her arms right. I know I'm going back to Jupiter next year. I refuse to be at the same club as Kshid-da—he'll pull me up in front of people—I can't take that.'

'I'll go back with you.'

The two of them spared another glance for Koni as they began to walk away. Then Amiya laughed. 'Once she's in the competitions, she'll be choking on the water I kick up with my feet.'

* * *

It was nearly a quarter to ten. He would definitely be late returning from the market today. Kshitish was hurrying down the road, followed by Koni. An Austin came to a stop beside them and Bishtu Dhar's face appeared at the window.

'Kshitish-babu! Just the person I was looking for. I can't quite get on top of that speech you wrote for me—it would be nice if we could discuss it. The meeting's this evening.'

'But I have to go home right away via the market.'

'Get into the car. I'll take you to the market and drop you home, and then we can have our discussion.'

Bishtu Dhar swung open a door. Kshitish was about to get in when he felt a tug on his sleeve.

'My breakfast!'

'Oh—your eggs and bananas.' Kshitish was disconcerted.

'Why don't you give me the money? I'll buy it.'

Kshitish silently handed over a rupee to Koni, adding, 'Be on time in the evening.'

As the car began moving, Bishtu Dhar asked, 'Who's the girl?'

Kshitish smiled. 'My future.'

* * *

As usual, Lilabati had locked up the house and left.

Instead of starting his kitchen duties, Kshitish sat down with Bishtu Dhar on the verandah. As Bishu and Khushi came forward to greet him, Bishtu shrunk against the wall. 'Shoo them away. I get all squeamish with cats.'

At a short command, the two cats left the verandah.

'That's magnificent training!'

'I love them, that's why they listen to me. One can do anything with love, even with people.'

'How can you equate humans and animals!'

'No, why should I. People get all squeamish about animals, but I don't know how animals feel about people.'

'There you go again, twisting words,' said Bishtu Dhar, extracting the speech from his pocket. 'I've highlighted some parts. It's the final of a street rubber-ball tournament—the chief guest is Binod Bhar. So his boys will be there . . . if they suddenly pose a sticky question and I can't answer, it will be very humiliating.'

Kshitish studied the paper. 'So what do you want clarified?'

'You've written: "Talent is god-given. It can be aided to blossom, but it can't be substituted. And if talent is not used, its possessor must be deemed a criminal." But you know what, I think there are many talented people in our country who waste themselves, fretting about food and clothing. Even you'll admit—one has to survive, right?'

Kshitish nodded.

'In Russia, for instance, the top sportsmen don't have

to worry about the basics. The government acknowledges their importance and takes care of them. If our government did the same, our athletes would be relieved of some major worries. One has to say these things, you understand—the public is now Left-leaning.'

'But neither India nor Bengal are Communist countries, we are democracies. All sportsmen have to fight for everything. That is the liberty a democracy bestows—the liberty to fight.'

'You want sportsmen to fight for everything—even food and clothing—like animals?'

'Not as a human being, but as a swimming coach, yes, definitely. Not everything comes easy, you know. Tell your audience that a swimmer needs to work hard, writhe in pain, before he can grow. Go on, read the speech.'

An agitated Kshitish began pacing the verandah. Bishtu Dhar cast one agonized eye at him and another at the cats, then he began reading: 'The glory of star sportsmen irradiates the whole country. If I ask you who comes to mind at the mention of Australia, the answer must be Don Bradman, Dawn Fraser and Ken Rosewall. If I ask you the name of the Brazilian prime minister, would anyone be able to answer? But you have all heard of Pele. Ethiopia is a tiny, impoverished, unknown country. But when Bikila ran his race, the country became famous.'

Bishtu Dhar paused to take a breath. Kshitish was listening to him intently. He continued, 'A medal doesn't do you or me any good. A medal is insignificant in itself, but it is symbolically valuable to a country, a people. A hero—be it a swimmer or an army General—is an idol for the children of the country. But even there, there's a distinction. A great swimmer stands for life and living, a General for death and destruction. A swimmer is far greater than a General. An all-conquering General is respected and hated in equal measure. But a great swimmer inspires the whole world.

'You're just going on about swimmers—why aren't you talking about footballers and cricketers? I have to cater to the Bengali audience.'

'You can talk about whichever sport you want to. But you must mention that we ignore those who infuse us with life. We forget that they need food and shelter, even if it's a thatched shelter. We force them into a miserable existence. We are the ones who teach them to be cunning, to lie . . . Say all this, then move into your usual tirade against the government.'

'Write it out for me, please. I'm getting all confused.'

Kshitish frowned. Bishtu added hurriedly, 'I'll pay your fees, of course.'

'I don't want a fee, I want a job. Any job, anything that earns me around 150 rupees a month.'

'A job!' Bishtu Dhar was astounded. 'Where will I get a job!'

'You run a business, don't you? I need a regular income. I can't depend on writing speeches all my life.'

'Okay, let me see.'

Kshitish had the speech ready in half-an-hour. After Bishtu Dhar had left, he loaded the cooker, then began setting up a rubber pulley in the yard. Two rubber belts hung from two large hooks, ending in two rings. Koni would work out on the pulley. That done, he began stuffing two small gunny sacks with sand. Koni would use these as weights for her freehand exercises.

On her return, Lilabati was surprised to see what Kshitish was up to. 'How come you've dragged these out again?'

'These are for Koni.'

'Koni who?'

'A girl. I'm going to train her. She's got potential. She's unmoulded clay, if I do it right, she'll be an excellent swimmer. She's very poor.'

Lilabati went in. Standing near the door, Kshitish said, 'She's very poor, doesn't get enough to eat. I was thinking of letting her have her meals with us.'

In a dry, hard voice, Lilabati answered, 'I've decided to rent the room. They've agreed to an advance of five thousand. Now we have to stretch every rupee, there can be no wasteful expenditure.'

Kshitish didn't push his point.

* * *

In the evening, Koni failed to turn up at Apollo. The next morning, she was half-an-hour late. Kshitish was going to rage at her, when Koni said, 'Instead of food, you could give me a rupee a day.'

Kshitish's anger was replaced by amazement. 'What do you mean? I should give a rupee every day for you to learn how to swim? Is that an obligation?'

'You make me work so hard and you won't feed me?'

Kshitish stared at Koni for a while and then burst into laughter. Koni joined in. They reached a silent understanding.

'You are a complete scoundrel. I see you've got the measure of me. Hang on, let me instill the joys of swimming in you, then we'll see whether you get into the pool or not. You say I'm making you work hard—the day will come when you'll be excited to work hard.'

Koni heard him out, a look of disbelief on her face. Kshitish noticed it and said, 'That girl you lost to in the one-mile race in the lake, her name is Hiya Mitra. Remember the name.'

Koni narrowed her eyes. She turned her face away and began adjusting the shoulder straps of her costume.

'Remember, Amiya has said she'll make you choke on the water she kicks up.'

Koni turned around. Her gangly body shook as she said roughly, 'I'll earn my costume in seven days. But I'm dark—I won't wear red.'

Amiya and Bela were working out with the kickboard some distance away. Koni was on the edge of the pool. Kshitish focused on her to the exclusion of everything else, his eyes reflecting approval, muttering, 'You scamp, you were pulling my leg all these days! Hang in there, I've got the perfect antidote–Hiya Mitra!'

'Kshitish, how is it going?'

Nakul Mukherjee came by. Gripping the railings, he said listlessly, 'You seem to be completely out of it. They've thrown me out of the BASA selection committee, all at the behest of Jupiter's Dhiren. On the other hand, Apollo isn't doing well financially . . . . If you get me one or two moneyed men, I'll make them president.'

Kshitish suddenly remembered Bishtu Dhar. He said, 'Okay, I'll try. But Nakul-da, why are you upset about the BASA eviction? A club is far more important than the state association. It's a club that creates swimmers; they are just go-betweens.'

'But the go-betweens' groupism, greed and infighting can ring the death knell for a swimmer,' Nakul Mukherjee said, adding with a laugh, 'Take it from me, no-one from Apollo is making the Bengal team this year, apart from those two girls.' He pointed at Amiya and Bela. 'And they, take it from me, are going back to Jupiter next year.'

After Nakul Mukherjee had left, Kshitish returned to Koni.

'Bend the knee, bend the knee . . . haven't I told you, the knee bends when you kick back, and remains straight when it breaks water.'

Shouting out the instructions, it struck Kshitish that Amiya and Bela could well be taking notes. What if they started kicking the same way! Then it occurred to him that they would never be able to abandon their traditional scissor-kick for this tougher routine. Even then, they could well pass on the tips to Haricharan. And he could train others.

Khitish beckoned Koni to the side of the pool. He whispered, 'Why aren't you following what I say? The ankle should remain straight . . . and when you kick, push back, rather than deep. That's how Schollander won four golds in Tokyo . . . Go on, do it again. Six beats, one circuit with the arm strokes and six kicks. Keep at it, keep at it.'

On their way back from training, Kshitish asked, 'What's up with your brother? Tell him to come by one day and check on your progress.'

Koni remained silent. Kshitish noticed her face become drawn and serious. 'Dada's unwell. He hasn't been to work for two days.'

'Then I must go and see him, maybe in a couple of days. And look here, we have to record your weight today. You have to start your exercise regime, increase your food intake. I have drafted training schedules and diet charts for you. I have to find out from the doctors about the vitamins you need. And if I can, I'll get the haemoglobin level tested.'

Kshitish paused as they neared the market. He had handed over a rupee to Koni and was heading into the market when she called out, 'Kshid-da, can you give me two rupees more? You don't have to give me anything for the next two days.'

'Two rupees? For what?' Kshitish knitted his brows.

'I'll buy rice. Dada can't go to work, so . . .' Koni fell silent and turned away.

Without questioning her further, Kshitish gave her two rupees—and realized immediately how the daily egg-and-banana allocation was being spent.

Kshitish landed up at Koni's home within an hour. Kamal was lying down on a filthy, torn sheet on the wooden cot, staring unblinkingly out of the window. His younger brothers and mother surrounded the pot of rice boiling on the stove. There was no-one else in the room. Kamal started as Kshitish cleared his throat and tried to sit up, but fell back weakly.

'Come in. Koni was just saying you would come by. But what's the point!' Kamal glanced at his mother and lowered his voice. 'There's nobody to visit. I'm done for.'

Kshitish sat down on a corner of the cot.

'What's wrong? Influenza?'

Kshitish laughed as if amused, 'Yes. But you mustn't linger—it's contagious.'

'You're on medication?'

Kamal avoided an answer, saying, 'Do you think Koni will be able to achieve something? She tells me what she's been learning every day. She's a very stubborn girl—if she says she'll do something, she will. If you can make something of her, give her a future—'

'It will happen. She's a bit restless to start with; if she can concentrate she'll definitely get somewhere.'

'I've arranged for one of my younger brothers to start work in a tea-shop. He's earning 15 rupees a month. I'm thinking of starting Koni in a cotton factory—they'll give 60 rupees. But then she won't be able to continue swimming.'

Koni entered the room and was surprised to see Kshitish. She came and caressed Kamal's forehead.

'I don't want Koni to stop swimming. I want her to be a great swimmer, to go to the Olympics. I couldn't do anything, now I want her to. You say she can do it?'

Kshitish said gravely, 'If she works hard, if she wants it.'

'You heard him,' Kamal raised his eyes to Koni. 'If he wants to, a human being can do anything. You have to break the Indian record. Then the Asian, then the Olympic. You can, can't you?'

There was a strange note of entreaty to Kamal's words. Discomposure, then subdued fear, raced across Koni's features. Silence engulfed the room, broken only by the sound of the rice bubbling in the pot.

Kamal asked again, 'You can, can't you?'

Koni nodded slowly.

{8}

Kshitish waited for Koni all morning at Apollo, but she failed to show up. She had never missed a single session over the past two weeks. Kshitish was now worried that she'd suddenly demand her swimming costume right away. He had continued to upbraid her, 'No, that's not right, the arms must not rise more than an inch above the water . . . why are the arms moving so much to the side—what's that, why aren't the movements synchronized?'

Even as he scolded her, Kshitish would think: I'll probably have to buy the costume today. Sometimes he would descend into the pool himself to show her a stroke. Others would swim around them; the hours would tick by, and Kamaldighi would become deserted. When Koni got upset, Kshitish would tell her, 'You agreed to everything your brother said! Do you think it's all that easy to climb up the victory stand? Breaking records is not like collecting mangoes in the Ganga, get it?' Then, on their way back, he would tell her stories of the greatest swimmers of the world, of their sincerity, their discipline and their hard work.

After a long wait, Kshitish finally left Apollo. Within 10 minutes, he was at Bishtu Dhar's residence. As soon as he saw him, Bishtu announced excitedly, 'Some people had just come from the Darjipara Boys' Library to invite me to be the chief guest at their annual social. Do you know who the president is? Binod Bhar. I've agreed. I'll deliver a fabulous speech and steal the limelight from him—he mustn't get any applause at all.'

Seeing Bishtu's emotions run high, Kshitish quickly thought of a plan. 'What use is a one-speech victory? Everyone will forget it in a few days. Rather, we should do something that will permanently deny him the spotlight.'

'How's that?' Bishtu was curious. 'How do you think we can do that?'

'One has to work it out—I've been pondering over this for three days.' Kshitish's voice was self-importantly low. 'I think you have to join the rivals of every organization of which Binod Bhar is a member. If he is part of a drama club, you have to join a drama club. If he is the patron of a religious society, you, too, have to make one of your own. If he is the president of a swimming club . . .'

'Yes!' Bishtu Dhar nearly shouted aloud. 'Binod Bhar is president of Jupiter.'

Kshitish nodded. 'You have to join Jupiter's rival club.'

'That's Apollo. But how do I join them?' Bishtu Dhar's tone was gloomy. 'Can you do something for me?'

'I'll have to try. In fact, I had a chat with Nakul Mukherjee just a few hours ago. He won't agree to anything less than seven thousand.'

'Seven thousand?'

'Well, one has to make a donation to become the president—it doesn't happen just like that. As a matter of fact, Binod Bhar is trying to fix up his brother's appointment at Apollo on the quiet. He has offered upto five thousand.'

'But seven thousand! Won't they settle for less?'

'How much can you bring it down? They already have an offer for five thousand. Binod Bhar is an MLA, there's a good chance he'll be a minister soon. Naturally, everyone wants to keep him happy. If you don't offer a higher donation, why should they take you on?'

'That's true.' A worried Bishtu Dhar began rubbing his tummy.

Kshitsh let a few minutes pass. Then he said, 'We mustn't delay too much—we need to finalize this in a day or two. Binod's people are really keen on the post.'

'Okay, I'll give them seven thousand. But . . .'

Before Bishtu Dhar could complete what he was saying, a servant came in to announce the arrival of a 'lady'.

Taking Kshitish completely by surprise, Lilabati entered the room. Though she was as amazed to see him, she didn't say a word.

'I've brought the money,' Lilabati told Bishtu Dhar with her customary gravitas.

A disconcerted Bishtu said, 'Come into the other room, your receipts and papers are all ready here . . .'

Five minutes after they left, Bishtu Dhar re-entered the room alone. Kshitish was bursting with curiosity.

'What was that about? The money?'

'Oh, something about renting a room. I have a house in Hatibagan, this lady wants to set up a tailoring shop there. She came to make an advance payment.'

'Five thousand rupees!'

'How did you know?' Bishtu was shocked.

'The lady is my wife. To take an advance from her is the same as taking an advance from me.'

A flabbergasted Bishtu stared at Kshitish's solemn face. He stammered, 'I didn't know that.'

'I didn't know you were the landlord either. Anyway, now we both know better. And knowing what we know now, do you still want to take the money?'

Bishtu lapsed into his stammer. 'Er . . . this is business. I do have a living to make.'

Kshitish stood up. 'I'd better be on my way. Binod Bhar would have left for the courtroom by now. I'll go and meet him in the evening.'

'No, no, please don't go.'

'Put up 2,000 rupees for the donation and 100 rupees for a nylon swimming costume, and I guarantee you the post of president at Apollo. But you have to return that advance. Besides, I will no longer write your speeches.'

Bishtu Dhar was shattered. He couldn't say a word, his eyes were brimming with tears. He nodded, whispering, 'I'm neck deep in this. If you desert me now, I shan't be able to come out.'

Bishtu Dhar left the room and came back with a bundle of 100-rupee notes. Handing it over to Kshitish, he asked, 'She is your wife, right?'

'You don't believe me?'

Bishtu made an elaborate gesture of contrition. Kshitish was walking away when he heard a plaintive voice say, 'What about my speech?'

'Don't worry, I'll write it.'

* * *

On returning home, Kshitish deposited the cash in his own box and began to plot. He would give back the money to Lilabati, but he needed something in exchange. And that would have to be for Koni.

As soon as Lilabati came back, she asked him, 'What were you doing there?'

'I go over occasionally for brainstorming sessions. Why were you there?'

'He's the one I've rented a room from. I'd gone across to hand over the advance.'

Kshitish yawned and stretched. 'If you'd told me earlier,

you wouldn't have had to make a deposit. If I forbid him, there's no way Bishtu Dhar can take money from you. In fact, he can return the money even now.'

'Why don't you ask him then? It's such a lot of money. It really pinched to hand it over.' Lilabati was eager to get back her cash.

'But I was thinking of getting Koni to have her meals over there . . . How can I ask for the money back in that case! If I'm going to make that girl slog, I have to do something for her. Now get me my towel, I'll go and have a bath.'

In the afternoon, Lilabati tried another tack. 'You're so concerned about that girl—she isn't even part of our family. But you won't lift even a finger to help me—I, who have worked so hard to set up that shop, saved and scrimped to expand the business!'

Kshitish beat a hasty retreat from home, only saying, 'Okay, let me see what I can do.'

* * *

He waited all evening for Koni at Apollo, but she didn't turn up. Then he bumped into Nakul Mukherjee.

'I've got us a president, Nakul-da. How much do you want as donation?'

Nakul was startled. 'What do you mean, how much do I want? Bot-babu gives us five hundred, that too most reluctantly.'

'Okay, I've got someone who'll give two thousand.'

After relishing every bit of Nakul Mukherjee's reaction, Kshitish told him all about Bishtu Dhar. 'Don't worry, the money will come. But I need full training facilities for that girl.'

Nakul Mukherjee nodded vigorously, beaming from ear to ear, 'Of course.'

After leaving Apollo, Kshitish thought he should go and see why the girl had stayed away. She was just too much of a shirker. She refused to work hard without a bait. But she had one Achilles' heel: her pride. Kshitish frequently recalled the way an empty-handed Koni had paused on her way out of Rabindra Sarovar after the competition to hear the name of the winner. In that moment, the humiliated girl who couldn't face her brother had blazed in fury.

There were no lights in the slum. Kshitish had some trouble locating the shanty. Finally, a young boy showed him the way. A lone lamp was burning in the room. Koni's younger brothers were fast asleep on the floor. The figure on the wooden cot was probably her mother.

'Koni,' Kshitish called out.

The girl emerged silently.

'What's the matter! Why didn't you come today? If you continue to bunk like this, I'll have to tell your brother that you won't amount to anything at all!' Kshitish berated her loudly.

Koni stood there, not uttering a word. It was impossible to make out her expression in the dark.

Suddenly, a shrill voice piped up from behind Kshitish. 'What sort of a man are you, pulling up a girl like that just hours after her brother has died?'

For a minute, Kshitish couldn't believe his ears. He looked back and asked, 'Who died?'

'So you don't know! Last evening he began spitting blood, by nightfall he was gone. Koni's brother!'

Kshitish shuddered. Then he heard Koni speaking very calmly, tiredly, 'Kshid-da, how will we survive now?'

{9}

Kshitish screamed in rage, 'You have to do it, you have to! I'm not listening to any excuses.' He picked up a stone and flung it at Koni.

'Please, Kshid-da, I can't anymore.'

'I'll break your skull . . . Die, why don't you die?' Kshitish looked around but couldn't find another stone to lob. Then he spotted the narrow strip of bamboo resting against the gardener's quarters.

'Kshid-da, I just can't.'

Kshitish jumped over the railing and picked up the bamboo strip. Koni had swum close to the edge. Kshitish grasped the bamboo strip in both hands and brought it down forcefully on the water. It came down about two arm-lengths away from Koni. He raised the strip and hit the water again.

'I'll break your skull. I'll kill you if you come out. Two hundred metres to go.'

As soon as Koni began swimming towards the starting platform on the western periphery, Kshitish picked up the bamboo strip and ran up the bank. Koni hesitated, warily studying the situation from behind the platform. Kshitish couldn't reach the platform, as it was at least 12 arm-lengths away and there was no connecting bridge.

'Kshid-da, Kshid-da, please let me go now. I'll make it up in the evening,' Koni whimpered.

'No excuses. No change allowed in the routine. I am not letting you go till you've done it.'

Koni hid her face in her hands and began to cry. Kshitish remained implacable. It was past nine in the morning. There was no one else in the tank. Some people lingered on the benches around Kamaldighi; pedestrians passed by on the inner pathways. A number of them looked curiously at Kshitish; some even drew up close to watch the scene play out.

Koni swam—from the western platform to the eastern. Kshitish followed her along the perimeter, bamboo strip in hand. There was no guarantee she wouldn't come out of the pool as soon as she reached the other side.

It was as if someone else was raising her tired arms from the water and dropping them back again. When she turned her face to breathe in huge gulps of air, her eyes appeared to close over in sleep. Clutching the stopwatch dangling around his neck, Kshitish kept muttering to himself: 'I know, I know you're hurting, your arms and legs are falling apart, your heart is about to burst. Never mind, you have to overcome the pain. Now you know how it feels like when hunger strikes, when it tears you apart. You'll know what agony is . . . Fight, Koni, fight–

'. . . Push yourself through training, Koni. Dare your pain: "Can you make me cry, can you scare me?" Turn on me, Koni, say aloud, "Kshid-da, I'll kill you, you're a beast, I'll tear you apart." Let your rage bring Kamaldighi to a boil.

'–Another 50 metres to go, Koni, let the agony hone your body. You'll see how it surprises you, this body of yours, how it will make the impossible possible. What's a gold medal–just a disc. It's what it symbolizes that's important–human beings can do anything, everything.'

Having reached the end of her course, Koni panted as she held on to the platform with both hands. Fleetingly, she turned to look at Kshitish, her eyes brimming with hate and anger. He noticed. After returning the bamboo strip where he had found it, he retired to the clubhouse and pulled out a thick notebook. This was Koni's logbook. Besides the workout specifics of each training session, it recorded her food consumption, weight, heartbeat and haemoglobin levels as well as iron and vitamin intake.

While making his notes, Kshitish observed an agitated Koni leave the club premises. Usually, she popped in to say goodbye. But not today. From the club, Koni usually went to Kshitish's home for a meal. Exactly at 10 a.m., she had to be at Prajapati to pull up the shutters, clean the premises, fill the earthenware pot with drinking water and run around on odd jobs, according to the deal made between Lilabati and Kshitish. In the afternoon, she would return to Kshitish's for lunch. Then, after a two-hour nap, she would work out for 15 minutes and go back to Apollo. After another round of training, she would go back to Prajapati. Once the shop closed its doors for the day, she would come back with Lilabati and have her dinner with them before returning home to the slum where her mother and brothers lived. Koni was paid 40 rupees for her services.

That day, though, she was running late. Skipping her morning meal at Kshitish's, she almost raced to Prajapati. Lilabati had already opened the store herself with a little help from the young man from the photography shop next door, who had pulled up the heavy shutters. As soon as she saw Koni, Lilabati pointed towards the street: 'Get out. I don't need you anymore.'

Koni paled visibly. With a customer coming in at that very moment, Lilabati said no more. Koni went about her duties one by one. Tiredness and hunger blurred her vision, forcing her legs to give way. She was dying to sleep, but there wasn't enough room in the shop to even sit. At one point, she timidly asked Lilabati, 'Boudi, can I go home for a bit?'

Writing down measurements for a frock in a large, thick exercise book, Lilabati said sternly, 'No.'

Koni slunk away to a spot near the entrance. If she was sacked, the family would lose the 40 rupees she earned.

After leaving Apollo, Kshitish, on the other hand, was making the rounds of one tailoring shop after another to buy leftover cloth. He had a deal with three laundries: They needed the scraps to mark garments received for washing. Kshitish had to cut the leftover fabric into even-sized tags and sell them to the laundries. If they bought three kilos of scrap everyday, he could make a profit of six or seven rupees.

Around one p.m., weighed down by a heavy bag of fabric, Kshitsh arrived at Koni's home. As soon as Koni's mother emerged, he snarled, 'When did Koni go to bed last night?'

'Why, at the same time as every day,' Koni's mother answered timidly.

'Is that the truth?' Kshitish glared at her. 'Why did she tire so easily today? If you lie to me, woman, you will be caught. Tell me again, when did she go to bed?'

'No sir, I won't lie to you. Koni went to watch a play last night. She went to bed around one in the morning.'

'Hmm.' Kshitish gave her the bag and said, 'Work on this tonight. Send it to the club with Koni tomorrow morning.'

Handing over five rupees to the woman, he said feelingly, 'At her age, she *will* want to do these things. But you need to be strict with her for her own good. Any sport is a matter of dedication. To achieve her aim, she must live the life of an ascetic. So many distractions come in the way. She'll get to watch her plays, of course, but not at the cost of her rest during this training period. You have to understand.'

* * *

Back home, Lilabati was waiting for him. Sitting down to dinner right away, he asked casually, 'Has Koni eaten?'

'It's impossible to get any work out of her,' Lilabati said after a pause. 'She's drowsy all day. I don't let her sit, but she was sleeping on her feet today.'

'I made her work really hard this morning.'

'What good is that to me? You save me 5000 rupees, and squander it elsewhere.'

'I pay 50 rupees for her meals every month, don't I?'

'Milk, eggs, honey every day—do you think 50 rupees covers such expenses!'

Kshitish finished his lunch quickly. Inside, he saw Koni fast asleep on the floor, cradling her head on her arms instead of using a pillow. Sitting down beside her, Kshitish began running his fingers through her hair. A little later, Koni curled up closer to him and muttered something under her breath. Kshitish leaned closer to listen.

'Dada?'

'Yes.'

A sliver of a smile passed over Koni's face. 'You'd promised to take me to see crocodiles.'

'Of course, I will—I'll take you to the zoo,' Kshitish murmured. 'And to so many other places too—Belur Math,

Bandel church, Diamond Harbour, the museum, so many places. Then you'll go to Delhi, Bombay, Madras, and even further, to Tokyo, London, Berlin, Moscow, New York.'

Even in sleep, Koni's face brightened.

'Kshid-da works me like a slave, Dada. I promise I'll win a medal for you.'

Koni went back to sleep, a smile lingering on her face. Kshitish continued to caress her hair. 'I'll make you work harder, even harder,' he said.

* * *

Prajapati was closed on Sundays. Koni, too, was off training. Kshitish had a bag slung across his shoulders. It contained rotis, aloo chhenchhki, jaggery, boiled eggs and bananas.

The two of them had left home at 10 a.m. After walking around the zoo for three hours, they settled down by a pond. Pulling out the two packages of food, Kshitish said, 'What shall we do about water? We should have brought a water bottle.'

A little distance away, a noisy bunch of 30-odd schoolgirls had arrived for a picnic. With them were four teachers and two staff members with baskets of food. They sat down in a circle for lunch. Koni glanced at them curiously once or twice, chewing on her roti.

'Kshid-da, they've got water with them. Shall I ask for some?'

'How do you know?'

'There, see that big barrel?'

'Try, then.'

Koni walked across to the teacher who was standing near the barrel. Kshitish noticed that as soon as Koni said something, the teacher gave her a once-over and replied with a sharp retort. A discomfited Koni came back.

'So they didn't give you any.'

Her expression was like thunder. All she said was, 'That's a rich girls' school.'

'Is that why they didn't share their water?' Kshitish had a stab at humour.

'The rich hate poor people.'

Kshitish was a bit taken aback. How had this chit of a girl got such ideas!

'How do you know that the rich hate the poor?'

'I know. Dada told me everyone respects those who have money.'

'Let's get a drink from the tap.'

Before they had advanced a couple of steps, a girl came running up to them with two plastic glasses of water.

They turned around. And recognised the girl: Hiya Mitra.

'You wanted water, didn't you? Our Miss Nandi is just too strict and mean. I apologize for her behaviour.'

Hiya offered a glass to Koni. But Koni behaved very strangely. She suddenly lashed out at the glass, knocking it out of Hiya's hand and onto the grass. Not only Hiya, but Kshitish, too, was stunned.

'We don't want your water. Tap water will do for us.'

Koni sped away. Kshitish said embarrassedly, 'Now I must apologize to you.'

A hurt Hiya said, 'At least you can drink this glass of water.'

'Of course.'

Although Kshtish had planned to scold Koni very hard, he said nothing. Hiya, he had realized, was Koni's future rival. For four days, he had made the rounds of Ballygunge Swimming Club on the pretext of meeting acquaintances, to see Hiya's training sessions for himself. He had even noted Hiya's timings with a hidden stopwatch. Kshitish believed it wouldn't be right to blunt Koni's grudge against Hiya. Let her nurture it. When the time came, it would fire her and make her explode like a bomb.

So, instead of scolding her, Kshitish said, 'Do you know what Hiya told me? She said, that girl is burning up with jealousy because I beat her.'

After that, Kshitish noted, Koni was more and more reluctant to leave the tank when practising.

{10}

The inter-club competitions began well ahead of Durga Puja. Kshitish didn't allow Koni to take part in any of them, not even in the one hosted by Apollo. Though she was now almost matching Amiya's timings, Kshitish firmly believed that her time was yet to come. Actually, he had no intention of unleashing Koni before he had ascertained Hiya's timings.

Already, certain circles were aware that Kshitish was training a swimmer. So much so that if he visited Ballygunge Club, Pranabendu would instruct Hiya either to leave the pool or would work it out in such a way that made it impossible for Kshitish to note her speed. Hiya hadn't participated in any competitions either in the meantime, which worried Kshitish a bit. Amiya and Bela won every club contest and even the state championships.

One day, Kshitish clipped an item from the day's newspaper. A girl named Rama Joshi had swum the 100-

metre freestyle in the Maharashtra state championships in Bombay in a minute and 12 seconds. Indian girls traditionally hovered above the minute-and-20 mark—it was quite a feat to touch a minute-and-12 in that context! Kshitish further toughened Koni's training regimen.

The national swimming championships were to be held in Delhi. Led by Amiya, the Bengal team left for the capital after Durga Puja. They came back with a gold, two silvers and two bronzes. The gold was Amiya's, won in the 100-metre backstroke. Rama Joshi claimed six golds on her own, setting four personal best marks.

* * *

It was winter. The water level had dropped in Kamaldighi. Sweater-clad people now used the park for their walks. No one swam. But Koni's training continued without a break. A number of people had protested. But Kshitish had said, 'If she can do it, why shouldn't she? Training needs to be year-round. Practice is essential. The movements must become habitual, second nature. Otherwise it's impossible to increase one's speed. We swim only six months in this country, that is why we are where we are.'

In the meantime, Kshitish had taught Koni to swim the remaining three strokes. Combining freestyle, butterfly, back and breaststroke, Koni swam a backbreaking total of two miles every day. The reed-thin body now weighed 50 kilos.

The new year came around.

'Kshid-da, you'll let her take part in the competitions this year?' Bhelo asked from the platform one day.

Kshitish was busy trussing together Koni's legs at the calves, so that she could use only her arms to propel herself forward. He answered distractedly, 'The season's begun?'

'What do you think, the season's going to wait for you? It's been ages since the Corporation released water into the tank–'

Bhelo fell silent. Kshitish had raised his hand. Koni was in the starting position.

'On your mark . . . get set . . .' Kshitish brought down his hand, noting the time as soon as Koni had plunged in. Then he turned back to Bhelo, 'What were you saying?'

'The Haricharan gang is running scared.'

There was no one around, yet Bhelo looked over both shoulders and lowered his voice. 'You do know that both Amiya and Bela have gone back to Jupiter? Haricharan has drawn up a training schedule for them. Amiya has said she can't work so hard. Hari argued with her about it, saying, "If you don't want to be trounced by Kshid-da's girl, you have to start training hard".'

'There's no point. Amiya can't match Koni's current timings.'

'So then let her enter the Jupiter competition and clobber Amiya. Do you remember the insults!'

Following Koni with his eyes, Kshitish didn't answer. Bhelo said hurriedly, 'Anyway, I almost forgot what I came to tell you. I've fixed it up with another tailoring shop. They produce about half a kilo of scrap cloth every day, they'll keep it all for you. Here's the address, you must go tomorrow.'

After Bhelo had left, Kshitish sat on the starting block, turning the words over and over in his mind. Right then, he saw Dhiren Ghosh and Bodu Chatterjee enter through the west gate and approach him inquisitively.

'Kshid-da, you seem to be pulling out all the stops. How's the progress?'

Kshitish answered as detachedly as possible, 'Progress of what?'

'Your creation of a champion! We saw Rama Joshi this time in Delhi. She's fantastic. There's never been a swimmer like her in India.'

'Yes, her timings were quite good,' Kshitish replied dispassionately.

'How's that girl of yours shaping up—the one you salvaged from the Ganga?' Bodu Chatterjee tapped his snuff box against the railing to loosen the lid. 'Has she caught up with Dawn Fraser yet?'

'Almost there. She'll catch up tomorrow or day after,' Kshitish said, his eyes glinting mischievously.

Koni was working out on the kickboard. Bodu Chatterjee looked at her and said, 'You're pulling my leg!'

'Pulling your leg! She's been learning to swim for less than a year and you ask if she's equalled Dawn's record.

How can I joke at such seriousness? Let her best Amiya first, then we'll look at the big picture.'

'That's true,' Dhiren Ghosh said self-importantly. 'But she won't be able to defeat Amiya—this is her last season. She's getting married soon, and will leave for Canada immediately afterwards.'

Kshitish was suddenly all ears. If Koni wasn't able to trump Amiya, it seemed that his life's work would remain unfulfilled. He would have to remain dissatisfied forever.

'Then I guess Koni needs to measure herself right now against the Bengal champion to know how far she lags behind.'

'No, no, don't do that,' Bodu Chatterjee said hastily. 'She's still a beginner. It will be a setback for a young kid if she gets beaten badly. That will harm her.'

'That may be so. But at least she'll be able to say "Amiya defeated me".'

Later the same day, Kshitish informed Nakul Mukherjee that Koni would definitely be entering the Jupiter competition.

* * *

Kshitish now became even more alert, even more calculating, even stricter about Koni's training. He kept a sharp eye on Koni's lifestyle, sleep, diet and rest. Every month, he got a reading of her haemoglobin count and continued to increase her workload. He tested her against the Apollo boys. One day, he printed a large red '70' on a sheet of paper and put it up in the club verandah. If anyone expressed curiosity, he laughed, 'That's how long I have to live, so it serves as a reminder.'

Actually, it stood for 70 seconds. To ensure the figure always floated before Koni's eyes, he had put up a similar poster at home as well. Rama Joshi was their target. Koni would have to swim her 100-metre freestyle in a minute and 10 seconds this very year.

'Nothing is impossible,' Kshitish would tell Koni while dropping her home at night. 'We are racing against time. This clock is our enemy.'

Kshitish extracted the stopwatch from his pocket and held it up to Koni's eyes. Koni studied it carefully. She played with the key to check how the hand quivered ahead.

'If our goal is the world record, we have to clear our way by breaking smaller records.'

'Kshid-da, when will I break Amiya-di's record?' Koni posed the question suddenly with her ear to the stopwatch.

Kshitish laughed, 'Why?'

'She came to the shop this morning to order a blouse. In front of everyone, she asked me, "You're a maid here?" I was so embarrassed, Kshid-da. My handwriting's very bad, otherwise I could be taking down measurements. Will you tell Boudi, please? Then I'll practise my handwriting every day.'

'I will,' Kshitish said softly. 'You'll never conquer your

shame completely. You can only win part of the battle by moving to the other side of the counter. Ability is the key to success. Your real shame is in the pool; your pride, too. When you hone your ability further, you will make not just yourself, but me proud too; you will make all mankind proud.'

'All mankind?' Koni was taken aback.

Kshitish patted her on the back, then said seriously, 'Yes, all mankind. Man can fly faster than the speed of sound, race 100 metres in less than 10 seconds. Women have broken the minute barrier in the pool. Man has learnt to increase longevity by undreamt-of methods in the laboratory, on the operating table. The day will come when man can beat the speed of light, and live as long as he wants to. All these records that are being broken—on land, in the water, in the sky—these are all shots at freedom, at beating the hand of the clock. One day, he'll destroy all watches, beat time—'

'Kshid-da, it's hurting.' Koni groaned indistinctly. In his excitement, Kshitish's fingers had bitten into her shoulder. He removed his hand awkwardly.

'I talk a lot of rubbish. Do you understand what I say?'

Koni shook her head. As if reassured, Kshitish said, 'It's tough for you to understand all this now. When you grow up, you will.'

'But Kshid-da, you didn't tell me how far I'm behind Amiya-di's record.'

'I will, I will—we'll show them at the competition itself, who will defeat whom.'

* * *

Exactly three months later, Kshitish bellowed aloud in the club verandah, 'Wickedness, this is all Dhiren's wickedness. Why won't they accept Koni's entry? How can they victimize the swimmers because of their own rivalry with Apollo! You must protest, take out an injunction . . . What do they think, that they can do anything they want?'

Nakul Mukherjee, Bishtu Dhar and a whole host of others were seated on the verandah. Kshitish was pacing up and down. He stopped and faced Jupiter. 'How low they've fallen—how low those good-for-nothings have dragged the club! They're playing dirty out of fear. They think they can outsmart Kshitish Sinha.'

Bishtu Dhar whispered, 'All this is Binod Bhar's strategy. The public should know. Shall I call a press conference?'

Nakul Mukherjee slowly shook his head. 'A club has the right to turn down an entry. They say the last date's over, so they can't accept it. Of course, they never mentioned the last date, so they have a way out. Protests and injunctions won't do any good.'

'It's a question of morality,' Kshitish beat his chest impatiently. 'It's a matter of sporting spirit, of courage, of challenges.'

Nakul Mukherjee pursed his mouth in contempt. An excited Bishtu Dhar said, 'What about a demonstration? We'll stage a protest in front of Jupiter, in front of Binod Bhar's residence . . . maybe take out a rally–'

'That's too much trouble,' Nakul said coldly, putting Bishtu Dhar in his place. 'It will create a lot of publicity for Jupiter but won't hurt them in any way. In fact, people won't even remember it till the elections. Let's think of some other way. Kshitish, you're certain that Koni can beat Amiya?'

'Of course.' Kshitish gritted his teeth.

{11}

'Competitors for the ladies' 100-metre freestyle event, please come to your starting blocks.' The annual competition at Jupiter Swimming Club was always a lavish affair. The four gates in the middle of Kamaldighi had been closed off and a tin partition erected around Jupiter's section of the tank. Wooden galleries rose up around three-fourths of the tank. Behind the starting blocks were three rows of chairs for distinguished guests, beyond which were more galleries. On one side of the blocks was a table, where the announcer was speaking into a microphone, while five-odd time-recorders stood by. Dhiren Ghosh, with a badge on his chest and a few brochures in his hand, was busy looking after the important guests. Haricharan was the chief referee for the competition.

Kamaldighi was jam-packed today. A part of the gallery had given way under the weight of the crowd, depositing a few spectators on the ground, one of whom had fractured his arm. People lined the banks of the pool beyond the railings. In the melee, two boys had been knocked into the water. It was just as well that both of them could swim. Many spectators had climbed up to the diving board. Beyond Jupiter's portion of the tank, that is, where the tin partition ended, began Apollo's jurisdiction. Around 2000 people crowded the railings here. They would see the competition from that distance.

It was the last day of the competition, beginning at two-thirty in the afternoon. After three events for boys and young girls came the announcement: 'Competitors for the ladies' 100-metre freestyle event, please . . . will competitors come to their positions? This is the second call . . .'

A solitary figure had so long been swimming desultorily near the edge of Apollo's part of the tank. The Apollo starting platform was about 50 metres away from Jupiter's. Sitting there quietly was a man with thick glasses and salt-and-pepper hair. No one had noticed him. Kamaldighi was overrun by people today, but everyone's eyes were on Jupiter's side of the tank.

As soon as the announcement concluded, Kshitish stood up.

'Koni!' he called out in his soft, calm voice. Koni emerged from the water and took her position behind the starting block. As one, all the spectators around the railing looked her way.

Swimmers were lining up at the Jupiter platform. Amiya was laughing in conversation with an elderly woman guest.

She appeared cool and calm. Bela had splashed about in the water a bit; she was now drying herself with a towel. The other six girls seemed slightly nervous. They tried to smile at one another, but soon gave up.

Coming up excitedly to Dhiren Ghosh, Haricharan whispered into his ear. Dhiren turned around and scanned the Apollo platform. Amiya followed his gaze. She had no trouble recognizing the black-costume-clad figure standing behind block number five. Next to Koni stood Kshitish, watch in hand. Suddenly, it seemed, all of Kamaldighi was aware that something electrifying was about to happen. Eyes were being gradually trained on Apollo.

Haricharan said something to Amiya, but she shrugged it off instantly. From the Apollo Club balcony, Bishtu Dhar's voice floated down: 'You have to show them, Koni.'

'On the board,' the starter cried, his air rifle pointing straight up to the sky. Eight girls ascended the starting blocks at Jupiter. Koni climbed up on Apollo's block number five. A buzz ran through the entire length and breadth of Kamaldighi.

They bent their knees, gripped the edge of the starting blocks with their toes, shoulders slung low. Their arms were thrust out behind them, like birds about to take flight.

'Get . . . set . . .'

Apart from Amiya and Koni, all the girls plunged into the water. The air rifle hadn't yet fired its shot. A round of boo's and jeers rent the air around Kamaldighi. Amiya looked at Koni out of the corner of her eye and immediately sobered up.

The rifle had been reloaded.

'On the board.'

The girls returned to their positions on the starting blocks.

'Get . . . set . . .'

The air rifle cracked.

Simultaneously, nine girls hit the water. At the same time, a quiet roar cascaded through Kamaldighi. The spectators stood up, as if they were watching a football match. Their eyes moved from left to right as they tracked two advancing swimmers 50 metres apart.

Upto 30 metres, Koni and Amiya kept pace. The rest were seven to eight metres behind. Then Amiya began creeping ahead little by little.

'Koee-neeeeeeee.' Somebody screamed out from amidst the Apollo crowd. 'Koee–neeeeeee.'

'Go, Amiya, go,' came the shout from Jupiter.

Kshitish stood as still as a statue, following Koni unblinkingly. There was no expression on his face.

Amiya had advanced by two arm-lengths. Bela was maintaining an even eight-metre distance from her. No one was sparing even a glance for the others.

Amiya was the first to touch the 50-metre board. As she turned and passed Koni, Amiya glanced back at her briefly. For a moment, Koni seemed taken aback. In the next instant, she had touched the board and turned around with the speed of a torpedo.

Like a feverish man, Kamaldighi was gripped by delirium.

'Koee-neeeee.'

'Is that a boy or a girl?'

'It's a girl, it's a girl—a member of our club, Koni.'

'She can't do it. She's a whole length behind. Why on earth did Kshid-da have to turn her into a laughing stock?'

Sixty metres. Amiya was still ahead.

Sixty-five metres. Koni was advancing.

Seventy metres. Koni and Amiya were shoulder-to-shoulder. Amiya was opening her mouth wide convulsively to draw in huge gulps of air. Her kicks were going haywire. Her arms were moving perfunctorily, as if they no longer had the strength to dip into the depths and drag themselves all the way to the waist. Amiya was burning low.

'Come on, Amiya, come on, Bengal champion.'

'Fight, Koni, fight.'

Suddenly, a great shout rose up to the sky above Kamaldighi like a rocket. Koni had left Amiya behind. Fuelled by the agony accumulated through daily torment, her slim body seemed to explode in the water. Her arms moved rhythmically, her legs kept pace; on either side, waves rolled away in a clean 'V'. The water she kicked up relentlessly followed in her wake.

Smooth, effortless, yet lethal, Koni pulled ahead. As soon

as she had touched the finishing board, she turned agitated, anxious eyes to the space next to her. Amiya hadn't reached yet. 'Wheeeeee,' Koni screamed sharply, turning on her back to kick the board and plunging back into the water in delight.

'Three lengths, she beat her by a cool three lengths.'

'Koeeeee-nnneeeee. Koeeeee-nnneeeee.' Three boys in the crowd were singing at the tops of their voices. Koni waved at them.

'What a show. Jupiter threw them out–they got their revenge.'

'Haven't had so much fun in ages!'

Suddenly, all talk, all excitement ceased, and then rebounded at double the volume. Claps and wolf whistles greeted an unbelievable scene. On the Apollo starting platform, the hitherto stone-like, unemotional Kshitish was jumping about, screaming, 'Haricharan, let's see you now!'

He continued, 'So you think you can fashion swimmers by lying about the Olympics? You need intelligence, you need diligence, you need devotion . . . idiots, idiots all!'

A flustered Bhelo came up to the platform and tried to calm down Kshitish. 'What's this, Kshid-da, have you lost your mind, creating such a scene in front of so many people! Come on, let's go into the club. Bishtu Dhar has actually fainted from excitement . . . Koni, come out of the water.'

Bishtu Dhar was lying on a bench in the club verandah. As he tried to sit up on seeing Kshitish, two people ran to his aid.

'I've sent for 10 kilos of rasagulla,' Bishtu Dhar said weakly. 'I'm calling a band. We'll take Koni out on a parade around North Calcutta.'

'Don't even dream of doing that. You'll lose at least 500 votes instantly.'

Bishtu Dhar stared uncomprehendingly at Kshitish. 'But I'm genuinely happy,' he murmured, half to himself.

Kshitish summoned Koni. 'Why did you mess up the turning?' he asked gravely.

'I got thoroughly flustered on seeing Amiya-di make the turn and get away. I didn't even remember the tumble-turn.'

'I think you lost faith in yourself. If only you'd remembered, your timing would have been even better.'

'What was my timing, Kshid-da?'

Kshitish dug out the watch from his breast pocket and frowned embarrassedly. 'I forgot! There was so much excitement as you were finishing . . . but I'm sure you broke the Bengal record. Damn, I wish I'd kept the time!'

'Kshid-da, I have to go to Prajapati now. Boudi will be furious if I'm late.'

'Yes, yes, better not hang around here,' Kshitish became anxious. But seeing Koni hesitate, he asked her, 'What's the matter?'

'Can I tell you in private?'

As Kshitish bent his head, she whispered, 'Haven't they sent for the rasagulla?'

'Of course! They must have sent Bhelo. In which case you might as well forget about the rasagulla.'

'Who says so!' Bishtu Dhar roared. 'If I can't take her around town with a band, then at least the rasagulla will do the rounds of town to visit Prajapati.'

'That will certainly placate your Boudi.'

* * *

On returning home that night, Lilabati fired her first salvo at Kshitish: 'Why did you have to jump up and down in front of so many people at this ripe old age? I died of shame. Making a spectacle of yourself—even the shopgirls saw!'

Scratching his head defensively, Kshitish looked over at Koni. 'How does your Boudi know?'

Koni whispered, 'Boudi went to watch. I had to tell her, or else I wouldn't have got the time off.'

Then she smiled. 'Boudi's taken my measurements, she'll tailor me a frock,' she said. 'She has promised me a silk saree if I set a national record.'

Walking Koni back home that night, Kshitish asked, 'What were you thinking, Koni, while you were swimming?'

Koni was quiet for a long while. Then she spoke as if in a dream. 'You know, Kshid-da, when I practise, I always think I see a face swimming with me under the water. I get so scared.'

'Whose face does it look like?'

'Dada's. He was there with me today as well.'

{12}

Ultimately, Koni did find a place in the Bengal swimming team. The national swimming championships were being held in Madras. At the BASA selection meeting, Dhiren Ghosh, Bodu Chatterjee and others in their group had protested violently against the inclusion of any Apollo member. Not content with that, they had also demanded that the club be suspended for 'unforgivable unsportsmanlike attitude' at the Jupiter competition.

The Jupiter gang had numbers on its side and was all set to get its proposals passed when, unexpectedly, Ballygunge Club's Pranabendu Biswas—Hiya's coach—said, 'Apollo should be let off with a warning that future slip-ups will be dealt with severely.' Then he added, 'For Bengal's sake, we need to include Kanakchampa Pal in the team.'

Pranabendu's words triggered an uproar. With Apollo unrepresented at the meeting, Jupiter had thought their proposal would be passed without opposition. Not in their wildest dreams could they have thought that Pranabendu would take up the cudgels for Hiya's rival. An angry Dhiren Ghosh said, 'Didn't you see what occurred at the state championships?'

'Yes, I saw,' Pranabendu answered calmly, his eyes not wavering from Dhiren's ashen face. 'I saw what happened.'

* * *

Not only Pranabendu, but others, too, had seen what had happened. Koni's competition came from Hiya, not Amiya. All three were swimming the 100-metre breaststroke. The championship's chief referee was Dhiren Ghosh. Among the stroke judges was Haricharan; the inspectors of turns, and the timekeepers included Kartik Saha, Bodu Chatterjee, Jogeshwar Bhattacharya and sundry other members of Jupiter's crony clubs.

Koni and Hiya turned simultaneously at 50 metres. Immediately, Bodu Chatterjee's red flag went up. Dhiren Ghosh ran to find out the reason and announced, 'Kanakchampa Pal is disqualified. While making the turn, she did an underwater double-kick.'

Kshitish was taken aback, but only said, 'There was no reason for such an error.'

The event ended with Hiya first, followed by Koni at six metres and Amiya at seven. Kshitish held back Koni from competing in the 200 metres. The breaststroke, which took a lot out of the legs, was just ahead of the freestyle event.

Koni was essentially a freestyle swimmer. But in this event, too, she was unsuccessful. After touching the finishing board at the end of the race, she turned back to see Amiya reach for the board. She looked up at Kshitish, beaming. Kshitish waved from the gallery, holding up his watch. The announcement, however, placed Amiya first.

Kshitish was astounded, then he ran to Dhiren Ghosh. 'What's going on?'

'What's going on!' Dhiren walked away, brushing him off, when Kshitish seized his hand.

'I've maintained the times as well. Koni touched the board first, her time was—'

'Keep your Japanese stopwatch to yourself.'

Nakul Mukherjee lodged a protest with the appellate jury. It was rejected. The 200-metre individual medley took place exactly 15 minutes later. Koni fell behind Hiya and Amiya in the butterfly, but caught up with Amiya in the backstroke. As soon as she turned, though, Jogeshwar Bhattacharya waved his red flag.

'What on earth is going on!' Kshitish raced down from the gallery. 'Dhiren, there's a limit to cheating. Jogu held up his flag even before she could make the turn.'

'Says who? Your girl made a faulty turn, Jogu held up his flag after that. Coach her in the technical points first—you've taught her nothing but to embarrass Jupiter,' an agitated Dhiren gesticulated wildly. 'Teach her the legalities—

you have to be on your back while touching the board in the backstroke. Kanakchampa turned and then touched the board. Now go away.'

Hiya defeated Amiya by a second. Two disqualifications and a first-yet-second outcome had squashed Koni. Kshitish grumbled all the way home in the bus, ending by saying, 'Let's see how Dhiren and his gang stymie you tomorrow in the 100-metre.'

However, Kshitish had no idea of the many methods of obstruction.

At the starting block the next day, Kshitish was a bit surprised to see the line-up. Playing by the rules, the better competitors were placed in the centre, in lanes three, four and five. Hiya was in lane three, Koni in four, Amiya in six. In lane five was Jupiter's Ila, who had scraped into the finals by coming third in the heats. Two years earlier, when caught red-handed while copying in the pre-university exams, Ila had bitten the guard.

Kshitish was going to approach Dhiren, when a volunteer stood in his way. 'No-one apart from competitors and officials are allowed on the platform.'

Kshitish came back to his seat, watch in hand. Competition was intense from the word go. Amiya was determined to bid goodbye to swimming with her championship title intact. Hiya was swimming smoothly, rhythmically, fast. Koni seemed to be an excited, anxious waterbaby in a hurry, turning the pool upside down in her quest for a safe shelter.

The rest were trying their best, but they were at least 20 metres behind these three. Ila appeared to be little less agitated: she was raising her face frequently and gradually inching closer to Koni's lane.

Koni was the first to turn around after touching the board, followed by Amiya. Breaststroke swimmers usually weren't good freestyle swimmers: Hiya was nearly two metres behind. The rest hadn't even crossed 40 metres. Koni had completed two or three strokes after turning, when it happened.

Ila barged into Koni's lane, face to face with her opponent. 'Uff!' Koni shouted aloud once, then they were seen locked together in a grip, each trying to disentangle herself from the other. A few seconds elapsed, during which Amiya and Hiya passed them by. Bodu Chatterjee waved his red flag at Ila, disqualifying her. She went back to her own lane and backstroked her way back to the starting platform.

Koni assessed the situation in a single glance. Then she inhaled a lungful of air and chased after the two girls in front. A lot of time had been wasted, but it was a last-ditch effort. Her arms moved like the pistons of an engine, her legs kicked up water until it seemed to be boiling.

'Come on, Pal, come on.' Cheering her on was none other than Hiya's father. His words snapped the gallery out from its stunned silence.

'Faster, faster, even faster!' The cry rose to a feverish pitch before finally breaking down in disappointment. Koni couldn't do it. Amiya retained her title. Hiya came second. Koni and Bela were tied at third place.

Then there was one more incident. Dhiren was leaning down to talk to Amiya in the pool, a big grin plastered across his face, when Kshitish pushed his way out of the crowd and kicked his butt. Dhiren landed headlong in the pool. A huge hubbub broke out. As a few young men dragged Kshitish away, he could be heard screaming, 'You can't do it this way, you won't be able to . . .'

Out on the street, Kshitish used Koni's towel to wipe his face. His mouth was bleeding. Koni's forehead had a lump. Kshitish halted at a paan shop to buy some ice. Just then, a car drew up next to them and Hiya's father disembarked.

'Sorry, Mr. Sinha. I couldn't have conceived of such a dirty affair. Hiya, her mother—no one is happy. There's no joy in winning such a medal.'

The gentleman patted Koni on the back. 'Don't be sad. You can now appreciate the importance of swimming fast. You're lucky. I'll never forget your last 40 metres.'

Kshitish was first confounded, then overwhelmed. Hiya and her mother were peering out of the car windows. Kshitish came forward to place his hand on Hiya's head and whisper, 'All the best, my child.' He hesitated and added, 'I scolded Koni very hard that day.'

At the bus stop, Kshitish ripped the torn pocket off his kurta. 'Don't tell your Boudi any of this.'

* * *

Pranabendu ran an eye over everyone present in the room. 'We know what happened. There's no point in going over that. We have to think about Bengal now, its honour and prestige—we have to put our insignificant rivalries behind us and build the best team. Only the Maharashtra girls stand a chance against us. There's no-one who can give their Rama Joshi a run for her money other than Kanakchampa Pal. The three freestyle individual events and the relay—of these four, Kanakchampa has a 60 percent chance in at least two—the 100-metre and the 200-metre.'

'How do you know that?' someone asked.

'From the way she finished the course that day. The stubborn, determined swimming she displayed shows that there's no-one in her class in Bengal. I keep tabs on her training, I've seen her a couple of times as well. That's why I can state so confidently that we need her if we are to snatch the championship from Maharashtra.'

'Will we become champions just by winning the freestyle?' Dhiren Ghosh said carelessly, looking around with a supercilious smile. But he elicited no assenting nods this time round.

'I expect Hiya to win three golds, two in the breaststroke, one in the backstroke. She has a 50-50 chance in the medley too. Anju, Pushpita, Bela and Amiya will win us points as well. We can be the women's champions this year.'

'But Kanakchampa Pal didn't take part in any club sports. She was disqualified in two rounds in the state championship, in the other she wasn't among the first two. And she didn't take part in any other event. We have no idea of her timings. How can we select her?' Dhiren Ghosh thumped the table.

For a few seconds, the room was silent. Finally, Pranabendu announced calmly, 'Then you have to form the team without swimmers from the Ballygunge Swimming Club. I'm withdrawing my girls.'

There was a sudden buzz in the room. Someone said, 'What's the harm in selecting her! She'll be travelling on her own money.'

Then ensued an argument, which progressed to yelling. At one point, Dhiren staged an angry walkout. On his way out, he said, 'Pranabendu is stooping to blackmail to get that Apollo swimmer in the team. I don't know what purpose of his that serves.'

Pranabendu replied, 'I have no purpose other than calling a halt to Rama Joshi's gold hunt.'

* * *

Koni finally got the go-ahead for Madras. The Bengal manager was Dhiren Ghosh. The women's manager was Pranati Bhaduri of Beleghata Swimming Club, while Haricharan Ghosh was the coach. They were to leave in the evening by Madras Mail. Kshitish came to the station to see them off. Kanti, Chandu and Bhadu were there, too, as was Koni's brother Gopal.

Koni sat hugging a window, talking to Kanti and the others. Kshitish stood a little apart. Dhiren Ghosh was supervising the boarding: it was nearly time for the train to depart, but a few people were yet to arrive.

Koni's face betrayed a faint fear. She had never gone out of Calcutta before this. And now she was going to travel a distance of 1,450 kilometres, for almost 35 hours. Amiya and Bela sat at the other end of the compartment. They were used to travelling: This was their fifth national championship. Hiya would fly to Madras with her parents two days later.

Koni continued to talk, stealing an occasional look at Kshitish, who refused to meet her eyes.

'Madras is right on the sea. But don't think of swimming there—there's a vast difference between the sea and the Ganga. The sea has currents,' Bhadu warned her.

'Koni, you'll face problems with the food. Idli-dosa won't suit Bengali stomachs—you must find a Bengali restaurant close by,' advised Kanti.

'Don't worry, we have cooks coming with us.'

'Are you scared?' Bhadu asked.

Koni looked at him, her eyes brimming with tears.

'Oh come on, girls much younger than you have gone around the world on their own. And you're travelling with a large group. Don't worry.' Chandu held her hand.

The guard blew his whistle. Kshitish was engaged in a conversation. He turned, saw tears streaming down Koni's cheeks.

'Kshid-da.' Koni said brokenly.

Kshitish pretended he hadn't heard.

The train had started.

'I'm scared, Kshid-da.'

Kanti and the others were walking along the train as it chugged along. Koni tried to spot Kshitish through the bars across the window, but failed.

A couple of hours later, the train stopped at Kharagpur. A curious Koni was looking out when, suddenly, Kshitish came and stood outside her window.

'Kshid-da!' Koni's scream shook not only her compartment but people on the platform as well.

'Remember, you must go to sleep exactly at ten.'

'No.' Koni shook her head obstinately, tears running down her cheeks. 'I shan't listen to anything, do anything. You're coming to Madras—why did you hide that from me?'

Noticing a ticket-checker approach, Kshitish stiffened. After the man had passed him by, he followed him out of the corner of his eye to note the coach he boarded. He said, 'Who told you I'm going with you—I'm going back to Calcutta from here.'

'Rubbish,' Koni clutched the sleeve of his kurta with both hands. 'Just try leaving.'

'But why should I go! Do you ever think of me?'

'How do you know whether I do or not?'

'Of course I do. You forget all about me the moment you plunge into a pool.'

The ticket-checker was coming back. Without waiting for Koni's answer, Kshitish slipped away, saying, 'I'll see you tomorrow morning at Behrampur.'

Haricharan, sipping a cup of tea at the entrance to the coach, told one of his group, 'I see that nuisance is traveling with us.'

But in the morning, Kshitish was nowhere to be seen. Sometime during the night, he had been picked up for travelling ticketless and was cooling his heels at the railway police lock-up.

{13}

Koni was lying down in a corner of the room. Her bed had a faded rug, a pillow and a cotton sheet to cover her. On a table near the head of the bed sat a small canvas bag. It contained a couple of frocks and her most valuable possession, her new swimming costume. Also on the table were her toothpaste, toothbrush and a hairbrush with half the teeth missing. Under the bed rested a pair of slippers.

As Koni lay there with her arms covering her eyes, the rest of the girls came back from their sightseeing and shopping trip around Madras. Koni hadn't joined them: she had just 15 rupees, which wouldn't buy her much. She had no desire to see the city either. The other girls refused to talk to her and had made it amply clear that she wasn't one of them. Koni, too, gave them a wide berth in return.

This morning, on their way out, Bela had suddenly quipped, 'Pranati-di, Koni isn't coming with us?'

'She doesn't want to, she says she's feverish.'

Koni was following the exchange closely from her bed.

'She'll be here on her own! Yesterday someone gouged out a whole handful of cream from my jar.'

'Oh Bela-di, my toothpaste tube was half-empty too. I didn't say anything, lest anyone think I am accusing them.'

'The room should be locked up, Pranati-di.'

'Then where will Koni stay!' Pranati Bhaduri's no-nonsense tone shut them up.

Shame and fear made Koni want to disappear into her bed. Every now and then, a suppressed fit of resentment seized her: so Kshid-da actually had gone back to Calcutta from Kharagpur! It would have been so much easier if he had come with her. So many of the girls had their parents escorting them. Why couldn't Kshid-da have come!

Hiya ran headlong into the room. Her parents, who were putting up in a hotel, had come by in the morning to take her out. Seeing the room empty, she came to a sudden halt. Then, spotting Koni, she said, 'I'm going to my father's friend, Mr. Sarangpani's house. Tell Pranati-di I'll be back in a couple of hours.'

Hiya's bed was on the other side of the room. Her enormous suitcase was bursting with things. On her bed were a pile of comics and a transistor. Three pairs of footwear were lined up under the bed. Chocolate wrappers were strewn all around. Hiya changed out of her frock and brushed her hair. Spotting a bar of chocolate in her handbag, she broke off half and popped it into her mouth, and flung the other half at Koni.

The chunk landed near Koni's chest. She threw it back at Hiya, hitting her.

A surprised Hiya asked, 'You don't like chocolate?'

'Why should I have it just because you gave it?' Koni said morosely.

Chucking the chocolate out of the window, Hiya said, 'I know why you won't have it.'

'What do you know?' Koni sprang up.

'I know what's happening here. You are suffering from a complex, that's why you are unnecessarily angry with me,' Hiya said, moving towards Bela's table. She unscrewed the jar of cream and dabbed a bit onto her cheeks. 'My father says Rama Joshi won't be able to repeat her six-gold feat from last time if you finish your 100 metres like you did in the state meet. But I don't think you can do that.'

Hiya scooped some more cream out of the jar and made her way to the door. Abruptly, she turned on her heels, came upto Koni and laughingly smeared the cream on her face. Racing out, she called back, 'Jealousy doesn't do you any good.'

Hiya's words worried Koni. She told herself, 'Why should I be jealous? Throwing about her wealth like that, giving me chocolate . . . who wants her charity! She's not mean about her own things, and doesn't see anything wrong in taking others' stuff either.'

Absent-mindedly smoothing the cream onto her face, Koni continued talking to herself, 'It's all about proving a point, showing people she doesn't discriminate between hers and theirs—as if I don't get it!'

Haricharan walked in. 'Oh, you're all alone. Where are the others? Such a bother—we had put up your name for four events, but it's missing from all four. They must have botched it up, I'll look into it. Tell Amiya to come and see me when she returns.'

Haricharan went out in a rush, just as he had come in. Koni sat as if turned into stone. After coming all this way, she wouldn't be able to take part in the championship! She couldn't think anymore. A sob built up deep inside, shaking her to the core. The vast, empty room slowly began reverberating to a muted, plaintive whimper. Only an occasional word struck a note of clarity: 'Kshid-da, Kshid-da.'

The girls came back arguing vociferously about the correct terminology for the Olympics: Was it the Mexico Olympics or Mexico City Olympics? No-one noticed Koni.

A sudden, shrill cry drew all eyes to Bela. Holding the jar of cream in her hand, she said frenziedly, 'My cream! Who's taken my cream again! Who? I'll find her out right away—there's much less now than when we left!'

Someone piped up, 'There was no-one in the room but Koni.'

Amiya said swiftly, 'Just check Koni's bag—see if she's hidden it away somewhere.'

Bela ran to upturn the canvas bag. Its meagre contents

landed on the floor. Koni stared at them as if she couldn't believe her eyes. The suddenness of events seemed to have robbed her of the power of speech. As Bela kicked away her precious costume, Koni protested and knelt down to retrieve it. Immediately, Bela grabbed a bunch of her hair and pulled her up.

'What this? What's this on your face?' The thrill of discovery almost asphyxiated Bela.

The other girls surrounded them. Amiya rubbed a finger on Koni's cheek, brought it to her nose and announced gravely, 'Cream'.

'My cream!' Bela shrieked.

All of them began to study Koni with the intensity of the sailor looking at a newly discovered island. Koni sat at the edge of her bed, her eyes helpless. The surprise of the attack still hadn't worn off; her lips moved but no words came out.

'Koni probably wanted to become fair,' commented one girl.

'Just as well, I'd thought Bela-di suspected me.'

'Now I know who was responsible for my toothpaste disappearing.'

'Hiya took out some cream and dabbed it on my face,' Koni at last found her voice. 'I have never used cream before.'

'What did you say? Hiya!' Bela slapped Koni hard. 'You're accusing Hiya? Do you even have any idea how wealthy she is? She can employ 10 girls like you as servants. And you accuse Hiya!'

'I swear, Bela-di, believe me. Hiya came in, and then left for her father's friend's house. She gave me half a chocolate, used some cream from your jar and put some on me as well.'

'Write a story, Koni, you'll be a great writer,' the contempt was clear in Bela's tone.

'Of course, we'd have to buy an alphabet book first,' Amiya commented mischievously from her bed.

'I'm telling the truth,' Koni's voice broke. 'Please believe me! Ask Hiya when she comes back.'

They didn't say much more. While they laughed and whispered amongst themselves, Koni sat stiffly against the wall. Pranati Bhaduri and Dhiren Ghosh came in. From the way they looked at Koni, it was evident that they'd already been informed about the affair.

'You should have waited till Hiya arrived,' Pranati Bhaduri said, addressing everyone in the room. 'Now go, have your lunch and get some rest.'

'Amiya, you have the 400- and 200-metre heats tomorrow. You don't have any competition apart from Joshi, but you still need to make good time. Bela, now listen: Joshi's in your group. You have to try your best. I heard a Punjab girl called Kaur is also setting good timings.'

After instructing everyone, Dhiren Ghosh turned to Koni. 'I can't figure out why your name is missing. They say it wasn't submitted. That's rubbish—they're trying to cover up their own mistakes. I've registered a protest, let's see. Whatever happens, you have to keep on practising. Don't be upset—the nationals are held annually, you'll come again next year.'

The girls were settling down to rest after lunch when Hiya returned. As soon as she spotted her, Koni—who had skipped her meal—sat up on her bed and cried, 'Here's Hiya.'

Bela held Hiya by the hand and brought her to her bed. 'There was a fracas today. Koni has accused you of being a thief.'

'What!' Hiya stood up angrily, her eyes fiery.

'Sit down, let me tell you the whole story,' Bela pulled Hiya down again.

'I know she's jealous of me. But I never thought she'd badmouth me like this.'

'We couldn't have imagined it either! We caught her red-handed after she'd stolen my cream and she said that you were the one to have dabbed it on her face. How foolish do you have to be to lie like that!'

Hiya was taken aback. As her fury abated, she tried to cover up her shock by saying, 'But I did rub some cream on her face.'

'Huh?'

'Yes, I used some cream from your jar, and I put some on Koni as well. What to do—I didn't have the time to ask your permission. I took some cream yesterday as well.'

Ending the issue, Hiya busied herself changing her clothes. Silence engulfed the room. After snatching a peek at one another, most of the girls pretended they were fast asleep. Koni looked at Hiya unblinkingly, thinking, 'I've been slapped, abused—all because of your whims.'

A nonplussed Bela had been quiet; now she directed her displeasure at Hiya. She said angrily, 'It's very wrong to borrow others' things without asking. You may be rich, but if everyone uses my cream . . .'

'Oh okay, I'll buy you another one,' Hiya said laughingly, folding her hands together, contrition written large on her face. Right then, Koni ran up to her and gave her a tight slap.

Hiya stepped back, one hand holding her cheek. As everyone sat up in bed, Koni slowly walked back to her corner.

'That was due to you. Ask Bela-di, she'll explain. It's because of you that I was slapped today and abused.' Koni paused. 'And I'm not at all jealous of you. I live in a slum, I'm not even educated—how can I compete with you? But if we ever meet in the pool . . .' She clenched her teeth, grinding out the rest of the words so that they were impossible to make out.

{14}

The swimming pool hugged the beach at Chepauk. Koni had never seen a pool such as this one before. Machines worked round the clock to keep the water so clean that one could see the bottom of the pool. Koni had heard that some posh Calcutta clubs had pools like this one.

The pool was surrounded on three sides by cashew-wood galleries and covered on top by coconut palm fronds. Next to it was the diving pool. Koni was a little uncomfortable in the pool initially, but it was only a matter of time before she rediscovered her element. In the past one year, Kshitish had been a permanent fixture on the platform whenever she was in the pool; now she felt lost slipping into the water without the familiar pat on her back. She couldn't quite figure out how to train. No-one seemed interested in her. Pranabendu was busy with Hiya. Most of Haricharan's attention was focused on Amiya. Still, Koni followed up a quick 400-metre freestyle run with several 25-metre sprints, another 400-metre, five minutes of turns and starts, and ended with a 200-metre medley.

A girl in a swimming costume was watching her train from the starting block. When Koni passed her by on her way out from the pool, she smiled.

'What's your name?' she asked in English.

'My name is Kanakchampa Pal.'

'You have a beautiful style.'

Koni landed in a spot: to avoid answering in English, she smiled back. The girl pointed to Hiya. 'Is she a freestyle swimmer?'

'What did you say?' Koni asked in broken Hindi.

The girl repeated her question in Hindi.

'I am. She's a medallist in the breaststroke. What's your stroke?' Koni replied in her uneven Hindi.

The girl smiled. 'Rama Joshi.'

Now Koni took a proper look at the girl. Dusky, slim, hair to the shoulders—she looked like any regular Bengali girl. Suddenly, the figure '70' floated up before her eyes. Koni walked away rapidly towards the dressing rooms.

* * *

Hiya was the first to win Bengal a gold. There were no more than five girls to swim the 200-metre breaststroke, so there had been no need for heats. Hiya's time was three minutes and 32 seconds.

Koni was seated in the gallery designated for participants. She saw Hiya ascend the victory stand with two others. A local minister presented her with a medal. The band struck up a tune. Koni experienced a wrench like she had never known. Hiya's parents were seated on the far side. She ran to them. Her father caught her up and kissed her; her mother pulled her into a hug. Wrapping her towel around herself, Hiya came back, and was immediately surrounded by the others.

'Let's see the medal.'

'Congrats, Hiya.'

'Thank you.'

'That was an excellent finish. Gujarat was running neck-and-neck with you—I was thinking if Hiya messed up the turn then—'

'That's the only time I was scared, my turns are so bad.'

'Did you see the Mysore girl? She always had her face out of the water.'

Koni continued to sit on her own. Hiya spotted her as she swept the gallery with her eyes a couple of times. There was only one final today, the rest were freestyle heats. Amiya had made it to the finals of all three events, Bela would compete in the 200-metre and Hiya in the 100-metre. It had been decided that Hiya would compete in the 200-metre and 400-metre as well but, at the last moment, Pranabendu had withdrawn her name on the grounds that it would harm her surefire shots at the gold in the other events.

Haricharan had argued with him. 'What harm could it have done? We'd have got two bronzes, two more points for Bengal. Bengal has a very good chance of winning the championship—and you, Pranabendu, are thinking only of Hiya, not of Bengal.'

Pranabendu flared up instantly. 'So I don't think of Bengal, only you do! Then why is that girl sitting there?' he pointed at Koni. 'Bengal would have definitely bagged the championship if she'd been part of the team. But you decided to victimize her to embarrass Kshitish Sinha. And you come pleading Bengal's cause! Now I'll keep a watch on how many points your girls win for us!'

Koni had no idea she had split the side into two warring groups. The next day, Thursday, would see the 200-metre freestyle finals in the morning, followed by the 100-metre butterfly in the afternoon. Amiya and Bela both went to bed after returning from the pool. Dhiren Ghosh entered the room, balancing biscuits and oranges in one hand, and a bottle of honey in the other.

'These are for tomorrow. Pranati, ensure that these girls have a glass of milk each in the morning. You have to be at the pool at eight sharp. Both of you should rest now. Go to sleep right after dinner at seven.'

After issuing his instructions, Dhiren ran an eye over the room.

'I just have one thing to say: Bengal has won its first gold today. We're on a winning spree, the last gold, too, will be ours; we will definitely be champions. Remember, lakhs, crores of Bengalis have pinned their hopes on you. They are waiting eagerly for Bengal to come back with the championship under its belt . . . . We've won a gold, we'll win the other eight as well. No one can stop us.'

The next day, Rama Joshi won both events. Amiya won the bronze in the 200-metre. The silver went to another Maharashtra girl, Sadhna Deshpande. Bela came fifth. If there had been a gold for screaming, it would have gone to Haricharan. Amiya tried her best. But she lost six seconds on her previous year's timing.

Amiya came out of the pool with a long face. Bela sniffled a couple of times. Hiya approached Rama to congratulate her. Then came the announcements, the victory stand, the medals, the band. Koni saw everything from a distance.

In the evening, the girls went out for a walk by the sea. Koni continued to hang around the pool. No-one managed to touch Rama in the butterfly event. No Bengal girl made it to the finals. Delhi and Gujarat bagged the other two medals. Koni watched the events uninterestedly.

On Friday morning, Hiya won the gold and Pushpita the silver in the 100-metre breaststroke. The bronze went to Gujarat. Halfway through the championships, Bengal's tally read 14 points, Maharashtra's sixteen. Hiya and Rama each had two golds. A frisson of excitement ran through the Bengal camp. Koni stayed away from it all.

Ahead of lunch, Dhiren Ghosh came around and repeated: 'Bengal is again rising to the top'—his right hand rose above his head, his voice reached a high pitch, 'in India's swimming table.'

Hiya's transistor was blaring rock music. Pranati Bhaduri switched it off, scolding her in a whisper, 'Listen to him, you'll feel inspired.'

'Keep the flag flying. We're running neck-and-neck at the moment, but I'm sure we'll move ahead.'

In the afternoon, Rama Joshi moved ahead of Amiya right after the 150-metre turn and completed the 400-metre course about when Amiya was making her last turn. Amiya had started the race recklessly, as if she was swimming a 100-metre. At the 125-metre mark, Rama was almost 10 metres behind her. Then Amiya began slowing down. Rama continued to swim at the same steady pace, stepping it up after the 300-metre mark and completed the last 50-metre, on her own. Punjab's Manjit Kaur picked up the bronze.

Amiya returned to the camp on her own in a taxi. On Saturday morning, Hiya had two heats for the medley and the backstroke. All eyes were now on her. Dhiren Ghosh had no speeches to deliver today. He shook his head, saying, 'No one expected such a poorly judged race from a veteran like Amiya. We've fallen behind by four points.'

'If only Haricharan-da had tipped off Amiya . . .' Bela said weakly.

'Anyway, what's happened has happened. Now a lot depends on Hiya. There are two heats in the morning, the finals of the medleys in the evening. Let her concentrate.'

As soon as Dhiren Ghosh had left, everyone turned to Hiya. Everyone except Koni.

Hiya cleared the two heats easily on Saturday morning. Rama Joshi wasn't participating in the backstroke. But in the second round of heats for the medley, Rama went into the finals with a two-second lead over Hiya. Immediately after hearing Rama's time over the microphone, Hiya left the venue with her parents.

The girls were talking among themselves in undertones. Hiya was lying on her tummy, listening to Hindi music on the transistor. For the past four days, Koni hadn't exchanged a single word with anyone. Amiya was alternating between lying on her bed, standing at the window and toying with things on the table. Pranati Bhaduri was reading a comic on her bed.

'Amiya-di, you should go to sleep.'

Amiya looked irritatedly at Bela and turned away. 'I have a filthy headache. That radio's really annoying me. Hiya, turn it off.'

Hiya showed no inclination to switch off the transistor.

'I'm telling you to switch off the radio.'

Hiya increased the volume a bit. Amiya screamed, 'Are you going to switch it off or not!'

'I'm listening to music,' Hiya answered quietly. 'Please don't shout.'

The sheer arrogance! A flabbergasted Amiya looked for support among the others. No-one responded; Bela, too, had buried her nose in a mystery book. The girl who had reigned as an empress over the Bengal women's swimming charts realized instantly that she had lost her crown to Hiya. Now she would be the centre of all attention, the recipient of all their adulation. Her own heydays were over. Amiya came back to bed. Were her days really over? Tomorrow there was the 100-metre freestyle, the 4×100-metre relay. Let's see if I'm really over the hill, Amiya thought, I have to show them tomorrow.

A little later, Pranati Bhaduri rose and switched off the radio. Hiya had fallen asleep.

* * *

In the thousands of watts of lights that lit up the pool in the evening, Hiya stood on the starting block like a still flame in her red costume. Next to her was Rama Joshi, after her was Gujarat's Ami Patel. As soon as the starting gun went off, Hiya burst into fire.

There was no match in India for Rama in the butterfly stroke. At 10 metres, she had left Hiya behind, breaching the waters with the grace of a dolphin. But as soon as she touched the board, she had to switch to the backstroke. Suddenly, anxiety gripped the galleries: Hiya was closing in.

'Go, Hiya, go!'

'Come on, Rama!'

There was as much ferment in the galleries as there was

in the pool. At the end of the backstroke round, Rama Joshi was still nearly four metres ahead. Next up was the breaststroke; Hiya was well aware this was where she would need to create and build up a gap. She knew she couldn't challenge Rama in the freestyle lap that followed.

With fierce power, Hiya's arms and legs pushed apart the water to bring her, first, at par with Rama in the centre of the pool, and then ahead of her for the first time. Rama, seeing Hiya pass her by, increased her speed.

The galleries were going mad. All the Bengal girls were screaming together, 'Hiya, Hiya.' Only a tired, unexcited Amiya sat quietly next to Koni, a strange smile playing on her lips. As if to herself, she said, 'Hiya will win.'

And she did.

Hiya started the freestyle round four metres ahead. Rama closed the gap by half at about 30 metres from the finishing line. Then began the do-or-die battle between the two. Rama inched ahead gradually. At the finishing board, the timekeepers leaned forward, with their stopwatches in hand. In the galleries, the crowd craned their necks to catch the finish.

Within half a second of Hiya touching the finishing board, Rama's hand reached out.

'I said so,' Amiya said, again to herself.

After the wait for the decision, as the others held Hiya and cried with joy, only Koni spotted tears in Amiya's eyes.

Bengal was now two points behind. Hiya and Rama each

had three golds. An excited Dhiren Ghosh announced at dinner: 'Hiya will win another gold tomorrow morning. Bengal will move ahead.'

'Dhiren-da, don't forget, there'll be two freestyle events after that,' said Amiya while playing with her food, adding carelessly, 'Rama Joshi holds the India record.'

On Sunday morning, Amiya didn't go to the venue. When the girls came back, shouting triumphantly, she was quietly writing a letter. Without raising her head, she said, 'So Hiya's got four.'

'Amiya-di, it was magnificent—Anju missed a bronze by a whisker.'

'Amiya-di, won't you be able to beat Joshi?'

'Amiya-di, everyone's now saying that the championship depends on you. Bengal and Maharashtra have the same number of points.'

Koni had torn one of her slippers, she was trying to fix it with a safety-pin. The excitement didn't touch her.

Amiya quit writing. 'I'll try,' she said.

* * *

It was the last day of the national swimming meet. There were just six events in the evening. The first was the girls' 100-metre freestyle final. Of the eight contestants, Rama, Amiya and Hiya took up the central lanes. The galleries were overflowing today. Koni sat there, barefoot. The safety-pin hadn't worked.

Amiya plunged into the pool before the starting gun went off. The second time around, Maharashtra's Sadhna Deshpande and Hiya had false starts. Finally, all eight managed to time themselves with the gun. At 30 metres, two figures pulled ahead: Rama and Amiya. Then Amiya used all her power to leave Rama behind. After the turn, she was a metre ahead. Hiya was lagging a little behind Rama, next to her was Sadhna. Haricharan had doubled over, screaming.

An indistinct moan rent the air. Amiya was floating in the water, clutching her stomach. Her face was distorted in pain.

'Cramps, she's got the cramps.'

Two people jumped into the pool. Bengal officials ran to the spot. Haricharan collapsed, head in his hands. Rama Joshi, meanwhile, had touched the finishing board, followed by Hiya and Sadhna.

Maharashtra was now three points ahead. Unless Bengal scored 10 points by winning the last event—the 4×100-metre relay—there was no way it could be the champion. Now Hiya and Rama each had four golds. With equal points, they were the joint individual champions. The relay points would go to the team, but the top individual gold tally would depend on who won the event.

The last event, the girls' 4×100-metre relay, would begin in half-an-hour. The boys' finals had just ended.

Amiya was laid down flat in the medical room. Outside

the room, Dhiren Ghosh was lamenting, 'So near, yet so far . . . So Bengal couldn't do it. Fate, it's all fate!'

Haricharan said heavily, 'Amiya can't make it. What'll happen to the relay team? There's just a few minutes to go. Hiya, Pushpita, Bela . . . who'll be the fourth girl?'

'In the reserves there's Anju and . . .' Dhiren stopped. Haricharan looked at him unblinkingly.

Pranabendu and three or four others arrived at the spot agitatedly. 'How come you two are still here? What's happening with the relay team, there's no time,' Pranabendu said.

'That's what we are thinking.'

'There's nothing to think about. Kanakchampa Pal must take part instead of Amiya,' one of them said roughly.

'But–'

'There are no buts, Dhiren-da. Bengal will still have an outside chance if she swims. Anju simply won't make the cut.'

'You two go on racking your brains. We'll take care of things.' Pranabendu sped away. Dhiren stared after him; then, like someone rising from a deep sleep, he raced after him. Haricharan stood as if turned to stone.

Koni, as usual, was seated in the gallery. The Bengal girls were milling around, whispering amongst themselves uncertainly. The men's medley relay final was about to begin. The contestants were lining up on the starting platform.

'Koni, Koni.'

Pranabendu and a few others were waving their hands. Koni wasn't sure whether they were calling her.

'Koni, quick, quick.'

Koni was too surprised to move. Dhiren Ghosh was waving at her. 'Koni, there's no time. You have to take part instead of Amiya,' Hiya clambered up to the gallery to take her hand.

A shiver ran through Koni.

'Me?'

'Yes, yes, you. Go put on your costume.'

'No, I am not going to swim.' Koni took her hand away.

'Bengal can't be champions then.'

'Whatever. I'm not going to swim.'

'Don't you love Bengal?'

'No, I don't,' Koni turned her face away. Pain and hurt formed a lump in her throat. 'If you want to love Bengal, go ahead. I'm poor, I'm ugly, I'm uneducated—I've had to hear so much. No-one talks to me. You cheat me out of participation, and now come to me because you need me—'

Hiya leaned over and shook her by the shoulders. Gritting her teeth, she said, 'I did not come to you for my sake. I came to call you for Bengal's sake.'

'No, you came for yourself. You want another gold for yourself, to beat Rama—' Koni halted.

Hiya was ready to slap Koni. Koni's hand, too, was upraised. Fire sparked in their eyes. Then, slowly, Hiya said, 'Koni, you're unsporting.'

'What did you say!' Like an arrow released from a bow, Koni sprang up. 'I haven't brought my costume.'

'I have an extra one.'

* * *

The speakers were announcing the start of the final event. The girls' team championship would be decided by the relay. The names of the teams were being read out one by one. There was a sudden commotion at the main entrance at this point. A crazed man had pierced the barriers put up by policemen and volunteers, and had entered inside. Two or three people chased him. The competitors had wet themselves in the pool, now they were drying off. Koni grabbed the towel from Hiya.

'On the board.' The starter's voice ushered in silence across the venue. Ascending the blocks were Maharashtra's Sadhna, Punjab's Manjeet, Bengal's Hiya and two others. There were just five teams.

'Get set . . .'

Flawlessly, Hiya and Sadhna dived into the pool. The cheers in the gallery began to rise to a crescendo as Hiya maintained a constant lead over Sadhna and handed over a three-metre advantage to Pushpita.

However, Pushpita failed to maintain the advantage for more than 50 metres. Maharashtra's Linda D'Souza stole an easy two-length lead over her. Bela watched anxiously as the Maharashtra girl dived into the pool from the starting block.

Standing behind the block, Hiya murmured, 'Bela-di, go all out, Bela-di, you have to fight.'

Bela fought, pushing herself beyond her limitations. On any day, any time, Dipti Karmarkar would have been able to defeat Bela by at least four lengths. But today was Bela's day. Dipti was unable to increase the two-length distance between them by even an inch. No-one had expected Bela to be able to maintain the gap.

Hiya was holding Koni's hand. Koni trembled like an engine about to start. All her focus was on Bela in the pool. As she was about to raise her foot to climb onto the starting block–

'Koeee–neeeeeeee.'

The foot came down.

'Koeee–neeeeeeee.'

The entire gallery turned as one to see two or three volunteers struggling with a man with dishevelled clothes, salt and pepper hair and thick glasses.

'Fight, Koni, fight!'

His hands were moving as if they were boxing. 'Fight, Ko-ee-ni.'

An eight-cylinder engine suddenly came to life. With a tremendous shake, Koni flared up. A stunned Hiya wrenched her hand away.

'Kshid-da!'

Hiya pushed her. 'Koni, up on the block, quick.'

Climbing up, Koni said, 'Kshid-da's here.'

Rama Joshi dived in. Three seconds later, Koni.

If the pool had been packed with earth instead of water, it could have been said a black panther was on the prowl for prey. Koni's prey was the timekeeper's stopwatch.

Just 30 metres in, the spectators realized something unprecedented was about to happen. They forgot to breathe, they lost their voices, they failed to blink. People rushed down from the galleries to crowd around the pool; the volunteers joined them.

Koni moved like a phantom through the water. Right after the turn, she caught up with Rama Joshi. Joshi sensed danger. She increased her speed. Koni kept up. For 40 metres, the two raced side by side.

Excitement swept through the spectators. Koni was nearly an arm-length ahead. Ten metres to go. Rama inhaled a lungful of air and concentrated all her power in her arms.

* * *

It was dark all around, Koni couldn't see a thing. A terrible agony seized her body. To throw it off, she repeatedly shook herself. Her body was dying to extricate itself from the darkness. She became desperate to make one last effort.

'Koeee–neeeeeeee.'

The long, musical tone floated across the water, nudging Koni. Like a child reaching out for a long-absent mother, she reached out and touched the board. She reached out and touched the board before Rama Joshi.

Koni was about to collapse right after Hiya and Bela pulled her out of the pool, when Dhiren Ghosh embraced her. The other Bengal girls came running. Rama Joshi tiredly patted her on the back and walked away. Koni was panting, her eyes shut. Concentric crowds had risen up around her; she was drowning in attention and adulation.

Then the victory stand. The medals, the music. Gold medal around her neck, Koni was walking back from the poolside, when she came to a stop. Kshitish was looking at her, his eyes blinking. There was 10 or 12 days' growth of beard on his face. He seemed to have shrunk in size.

'Where were you?'

'Tell me where you think I was!'

Koni's lips trembled, her eyes were swimming in tears. She turned her face away.

'Those idiots didn't keep your time; if they had, they'd have seen . . . what would they have seen, tell me?'

Koni ignored his words, growing angrier by the second. 'Where were you hiding? All you say is "tell me and tell me"!'

'Do you know where I was? I was right there.' Kshitish bent over and used his right hand to point at the pool. 'I was hiding there, in the water, and telling you–yes, one can do anything . . . fight Koni, fight!'

'Liar!' Koni ran up and showered Kshitish with little blows. 'I didn't hear anything, didn't see anything! I was dying of agony.'

'But that was me, dear child, that agony was me.' Kshitish laughed aloud uproariously.

A number of people turned around at the sound. They saw the girl who had just displayed such extraordinary swimming skills holding on to a crazy-looking man. She was sobbing into his chest, while his teardrops fell on her head.

Translator's Note

Koni had already passed into legend when I read it as an adolescent. And, I'm not proud of admitting this, I read it because the film based on the novel was about to release. I could read Bangla, but it was harder for me than reading English—and so, of course, I looked for every excuse to avoid it.

But the one thing I couldn't resist was a good story, even if it was couched in harder-to-access Bangla. And *Koni* had me hooked from word go. Koni, the young lead character, was a world apart from the Darrell Rivers or Nancy Drew I had known till then. In her story, I found a familiar reality, in her language I heard an echo I recognized. Even as my elder siblings raved about Kshid-da, Koni's coach, I was entranced by the girl who believed she could swim her way to gold.

So, apparently, were many others. When I met Moti Nandy a few months before his death, he told me quite a few Bengal swimmers believed he had based *Koni* on their lives. Nandy's inspiration, however, came from distant shores: from the story of Dawn Fraser (Google her!) and many other sporting champions who delighted spectators with their sheer talent and grit.

More than 30 years after Nandy wrote *Koni*, in a radically different world from the 1970's Kolkata he depicted, we can be still awestruck by a Sachin Tendulkar or an Usain Bolt. That is the magic which Nandy's genius spotted in sport, making him possibly the first writer in India to root multiple novels on the football ground, the cricket pitch and, yes, in the swimming pool. That's just one reason why his stories still ring a bell today. The others are for you to discover.

As I did, revisiting *Koni* for the translation. Nandy is a translator's dream, never using a superfluous word or wasting a scene. All I had to do was follow his lead. I've tried to retain the simplicity and economy of his expression, finding the English word or phrase closest to the Bengali one so as to not make the translation too 'exotic', and sometimes leaving the Bengali one to retain the authenticity and atmosphere of his writing.

Nandy passed away in January 2010, but I know that he was happy his stories were crossing the language barrier. This translation is dedicated to his memory.

Bangalore 2010 *Sumana Mukherjee*

{The Book Mine Gems}

Koni
The Story of a Champion

Extra-special pages to help you know more
about the book, the author and the author's times . . .

CONTENTS

AUTHOR REPORT CARD

NAME: Moti Nandy

DATE OF BIRTH: 10 July 1931

FATHER'S NAME: Chunilal Nandy

MOTHER'S NAME: Malinabala Debi

FATHER'S OCCUPATION: Doctor, served in the British Indian Army in World War I in Iraq

MOTHER'S OCCUPATION: Housewife

HISTORY: The youngest of four siblings, three brothers and a sister, Nandy was born in north Calcutta. His father passed away when Nandy was merely 17 months old. He attended Scottish Church School—a missionary school located along one boundary of the famous tank of Hedua. It is Hedua Tank that inspired Kamaldighi in Koni.

SPORTS: He played cricket and football, and swam in school, and this is where his interest in sports was born. He played club cricket in Calcutta between 1952 and 1956. Much of his fiction on cricket germinated from his stint as a club cricketer during this period.

SENIOR YEARS: Moti Nandy did not join college when he graduated from school in 1950. Instead he got a diploma in automobile engineering, and went on to work for the State Transport Corporation. In 1956, he enrolled for a degree in Bengali in the Maharaja Manindra Chandra Nandy College. In 1960, after his graduation, Nandy became a sports journalist and editor with the *Ananda Bazaar Patrika*, where he would eventually become editor of the sports section.

Political Science: Nandy wrote during some of the most politically volatile times in India, and especially in Bengal. Koni, for example, was written in the period just before Indira Gandhi declared Emergency, and all of Bengal was in the clutches of Naxalism. Nandy, however, mostly kept politics out of his sports writing. Through his life he was approached by various political parties to join them, but he steadfastly refused all of them.

Literature: Nandy has written over 40 works for both adults and children. His first published short story was titled *Behula'r Bhyala* and was published in 1957 in the literary magazine *Porichoy*. His first sports story was published in 1961 in the Bengali newspaper *Jugantar*. Nandy was able to construct a very attractive blend of literary skill and knowledge of sports, which led to him being acclaimed as an author for young adults. Among his early novels for young readers were *Nonida Not Out*, *Striker* and *Stopper*. Many of his later sports novels were woven around the very popular character, Kalabati, a woman cricketer.

Key Achievements: Moti Nandy was one of the most prominent writers in the Bengali language. He wove a vast web of stories that has kept his readers engaged for decades. He won the Ananda Purashkar for his body of sports fiction in 1974, just before the publication of *Koni*. He was also a recipient of the Sahitya Akademi Award in 1991. In 2008, he was given the Lifetime Achievement Award for sports journalism by the Calcutta Sports Journalists' Association. Of all his works, *Koni* was made into a film and went on to win the National Award for Best Film in 1985.

SHH. . . DON'T TELL ANYONE!

In which we investigate top secret files on Moti Nandy, and share some inside information with you!

- ★ When Moti Nandy was working at the State Transport Corporation (STC), he actually planned to go and work for truck manufacturers, Leyland, in England. However, he needed a recommendation from the STC, which never came. Just as well, or we might never have read his stories!
- ★ During his stint as a cricketer, even though he didn't have any ambition of becoming a sports writer back then, Nandy joined a group of writers, who met informally and read one another's works. He was writing every night, throughout this period.
- ★ Nandy's forays into writing officially began when a short story competition was announced in memory of the distinguished Bengali author Manik Bandhyopadhyay (a literary sensation in Bengal at that time and author of such novels as *Putul Nacher Itikawtha* and *Padma Nadir Majhi*) in 1956. Nandy entered his short story, *Nokhhotrer Raat* (Night of the Stars), and when the award was announced in 1957, he was declared the winner. This was the very first time his skill as a writer was acknowledged publicly.

- ★ Nandy's first piece as a journalist was an interview with Pankaj Mullick on Nari Contractor's head injury. Contractor was India's captain for the 1961–62 Indian tour of the West Indies. In a match against Barbados, he tried to duck a short ball from Charlie Griffith, but was hit on the head. He took the blow on the back of his skull, and was unconscious for six days, effectively ending his career.
- ★ As Sports Editor of the *Ananda Bazaar Patrika*, Nandy was single-handedly responsible for bringing the biographies of sports people and stories from international sporting events from around the world to the doorstep of Bengalis, who were a sport-loving people. He used the resources of the British Council Library, Calcutta, to research his stories.
- ★ Nandy's love affair with swimming continued through most of his life. It culminated in his eldest daughter falling in love and marrying champion swimmer Ashish Das. This happened after *Koni* was published.
- ★ Nandy was old-school when it came to his cricket. He refused to watch One-Day Internationals or Twenty20 matches. He only watched Test matches. He explained this by saying: 'I am a champion of individual skill.'

THE STORY OF THE STORY

In which we tell you what happened to this book, and share with you some of its best-kept secrets!

★ The immediate inspiration for *Koni* was Dawn Fraser. Moti Nandy had just then read a biography of the great Australian swimmer. Born in 1937, Fraser is one of the only sportspeople to have won three Olympic gold medals for the same event (100-metre freestyle). Like Koni, Fraser came from impoverished conditions. She was born into a working-class family in the suburbs of Sydney, and, like Koni, was discovered by her coach, Harry Gallagher, while swimming with boys at the local beach, at the age of fourteen. Fraser went on to win eight Olympics medals, six Commonwealth medals, and held 39 world records.

★ Nandy's school, Scottish Church Collegiate School, overlooks the Hedua Tank in north Calcutta. This was the inspiration for Kamaldighi. There were two clubs, the National Swimming Club and the Central Swimming Club, which inspired Jupiter Club and Apollo Club.

★ The year before Koni was written, a young girl named Ila Pal had won the 200-metre breaststroke in the state championships. She was running fourth at the first turn—50 metres—but swam an incredible race after that to win. The daughter of a grocer, her background was not very different from Koni's—who shares her surname Pal. But Koni wasn't specifically based on Ila, although Nandy often mentioned that Ila was convinced she was the model for Koni.

- ★ Nandy used a lot of real-life stories in the book. For example, during his research, some swimming officials revealed that because there were no forcible laws on lanes in the swimming competitions at that time, they would have someone collide against promising swimmers to sabotage their race, which is exactly what happens to Koni.
- ★ Kshitish Sinha was based on a swimming coach named K.P. Sarkar.
- ★ Koni was made into a hit film in 1984, directed by Saroj Dey, and starring Soumitra Chatterjee (famous for his portrayal of much loved characters like Apu from *Apur Shanshar* and Feluda from the iconic films *Sonar Kella* and *Joi Baba Felunath*) and Sriparna Banerjee as Koni.
- ★ Nandy himself had little to do with the film. He did write a new opening scene for the beginning of the film, in which Kshitish goes to villages, scouting for fresh swimming talent.

IN THE NEWS

In which we present what a newspaper in Calcutta at that time would say . . .

NAXALS CONTINUE TO WREAK HAVOC

Radical Communists known as Naxals after the uprising of Naxalbari, a small village in northern West Bengal, in 1967, have started to move into Calcutta. The intelligentsia, especially the radical elements of the student bodies at Calcutta and Jadavpur University, have been rumoured to be heavily involved with the group. Schools and colleges have remained closed in fear of attacks. Sources close to the Naxals have informed us that the retaliation by the police and Armed Forces has been brutal. They claim that more than 5000 students and intellectuals have 'disappeared', although the Government of West Bengal claims that they have all gone into rural areas to eliminate the 'class enemies' against their revolution.

RAILWAY STRIKE CALLED OFF

The ongoing 20-day strike by railway workers, demanding a 75-percent hike in wages, has been brutally suppressed by the Government of India and the Railway Ministry. Thousands of striking workers have been sent to jail or removed from their official positions, the agitation's leader, Mr. George Fernandes announced. The strike, which began on 8 May 1974, saw more than 17 million workers striking, making it the largest ever strike in the world.

India Carries Out Second Nuclear Weapon Test

Pokhran, located in the Thar Desert in Rajasthan, was the dramatic backdrop for India's first nuclear test. The code name of the whole operation was Smiling Buddha. This was the first test that was conducted by a nation that is not a member of the United Nations Security Council. The bomb was measured to give an explosive yield of 8 kilo-tons.

India Launches First Sattelite

In an unprecedented display of scientific might, India launched its first satellite, Aryabhatta. The Indian Space Research Organization (ISRO) constructed the satellite in collaboration with the Soviet Union. It was launched using the Cosmos-3M launch-vehicle, from the Soviet rocket launch site, Kapustin Yar. The satellite will aid ISRO in further astronomical study.

Sikkim Now A Part Of India

Sikkim has become a state of the Indian Union after years of struggle to overthrow the monarchy. Sikkim had protectorate status from India, with its external affairs, defence, diplomacy and communications controlled by the Government of India, while retaining its autonomous status. After 97.5 percent of the people of Sikkim voted to join the Indian Union in a referendum, the monarchy was abolished, and Sikkim became the twenty-second state of India.

Mining Disaster In Chasnala Kills 372

In a shocking mining accident, which caused a huge explosion in the Chasnala mines owned by the Indian Iron and Steel Company near Dhanbad, 372 miners have lost their lives. Seven million gallons of water gushed into the mines when the roof caved in, leaving the miners fighting for their lives under debris and water.

President Declares Emergency

After consultation with her cabinet, Prime Minister Indira Gandhi advised President Fakhruddin Ali Ahmed to declare a state of Emergency in the country. Under Article 352 of the Indian Constitution, Mrs. Gandhi will now be allowed to rule by decree, allowing her to make laws unannounced, and suspend elections and civil liberties. This has taken place in the face of Jayaprakash Narayan's continued agitation and satyagraha against provincial and central governments, to unify students, peasants and labour organizations to transform Indian society. There has also been large-scale protest arising from the allegations of electoral fraud levelled by Raj Narain, the main opponent of Mrs. Gandhi in the 1971 elections.

East Bengal Holds On To Calcutta League

In an amazing display of superior skill over their traditional rivals, Mohun Bagan and Mohammedan Sporting, East Bengal romped home to win the Calcutta League First Division for the sixth successive time. The club has been on a spectacular winning streak, and has been winning the League since 1970.

India Battered By England

In cricket news, India has had an appalling tour of England this summer. After four seasons of being one of the best teams competing in Test cricket, with successful tours of West Indies and England, in this tour, under captain Ajit Wadekar, India have managed a disastrous showing. India posted its lowest score in Tests: a pathetic 42 in the second innings of the second Test. The English routed the Indian team in both the One-Day and Test series. On their return from England, the team's captain Ajit Wadekar informed the BCCI that he would quit as skipper with immediate effect.

THE WORLD'S GREATEST SWIMMERS

In which we introduce you to the best of the best swimmers to have ever entered a swimming pool . . .

DAWN FRASER

Possibly the closest story to that of Koni's. At the age of 14, Fraser was discovered by her coach Harry Gallagher, while she was swimming at the local beach. Fraser won eight Olympic medals, including four gold medals, and six Commonwealth Games gold medals. She also held 39 records. The 100-metre freestyle record was hers for 15 years—from 1 December 1956 to 8 January 1972. She is the first of only two swimmers in Olympic history (Krisztina Egerszegi being the other) to win individual gold medals for the same event at three successive Olympics (the 100-metre freestyle—in 1956, 1960 and 1964).

IAN THORPE

Nicknamed 'Thorpedo', Ian Thorpe wrote his name in the history books, at fourteen, by becoming the youngest male athlete to represent Australia at the Perth Swimming World Championships in 1998. He went on to build an impressive career, winning five Olympic golds (the most by any Australain) and 11 World Championship gold medals. In 2001 he became the first swimmer to win six golds at the World Chamionships. In 2006, he retired from competitive swimming, and became a philanthropist.

JENNY THOMSON

Having participated in four consecutive Olympics, this is another highly decorated American Olympian. She made her debut at the age of 14 and went on to win 12 medals, of which eight were gold. She is currently a doctor in Boston, USA.

JOHNNY WEISSMULLER

Not only was he a champion swimmer, but he was also Tarzan! This Hungarian-born American swimmer won five Olympic gold medals and one bronze. Through the 1920's, he held 67 world records. Even after his swimming career was over, his name stayed in lights, as he went on to portray Tarzan in 12 movies!

KRISZTINA EGERSZEGI

In her first Olympics in 1988, this Hungarian swimmer became the youngest ever Olympic gold medalist at the age of fourteen. She participated in three more Olympic Games, with a career haul of five gold medals. Along with Dawn Fraser, she is one of two Olympians to have won the same event in three consecutive Games—the 200-metre backstroke in 1988, 1992 and 1996.

Mark Spitz

In the 1972 Munich Olympics, the 22-year-old Spitz won seven gold medals for the USA. This record was held by Spitz till 2008, when another American, Michael Phelps, won eight medals. In his career, Mark Spitz held 33 records, and is universally accepted as one of the greatest sportsmen to have ever walked the Earth.

Matt Biondi

Matt Biondi of the USA, is another all-time great Olympian. Having appeared in three consecutive Summer Olympics, 1984, 1988, and 1992, Biondi won 11 Olympic medals, including eight golds. In the 1988 Seoul Olympics, Biondi won seven medals, five of which were golds. After Mark Spitz, Biondi was only the second Olympian to do so.

Michael Phelps

The 2008 Olympics will be best remembered for the performance of this American swimmer. He won eight gold medals, the highest by any athlete in the Olympics. To date, Phelps has won sixteen Olympic medals. He currently holds 37 world records.

THE GREATEST ON-SCREEN COACHES OF ALL TIME

In which we bring you some of the greatest coaches to have graced the silver screen:

IRV BLITZER, *COOL RUNNINGS*

Played by the legendary John Candy, this is a heartwarming movie about Jamaica's first bobsled team (bobsledding is a winter sport in which teams of two or four slide down narrow, twisting and banked iced tracks in a sled). Taking his team from the heat and sand of Jamaica to the finals of the icy Winter Olympics, is Irv Blitzer, disgraced former American bobsled star. In this movie of unlikely triumphs, John Candy warms the viewer's hearts.

KEN CARTER, *COACH CARTER*

Coach Ken Carter, played by Samuel L. Jackson, benches his school basketball team after they break a contract with him. At the beginning of the year, the coach had made his team sign an undertaking that they would get better high-school grades. When they fail to do so, Carter drops the whole team, which causes the whole town to go against him. What happens next? Watch the film!

JIMMY DUGGAN, *A LEAGUE OF THEIR OWN*

Portrayed brilliantly by two-time Oscar winner, Tom Hanks, Jimmy Duggan is in charge of the first girl's baseball team in America, created because the men are away fighting World War II. The film is based on two sisters, who generate a heated rivalry within the team, and how their coach deals with the situation.

HERMAN BOONE, *REMEMBER THE TITANS*

Herman Boone (Denzel Washington), is the coach of a high-school American Football team, which is fraught with racial tension. The film is based on true events that occurred in Alexandria, Virginia in 1971. It is about how Boone, with his fantastic people-management skills, is able to overcome the problems, and take the team to victory.

KABIR KHAN, *CHAK DE! INDIA*

After a disastrous loss to Pakistan, national hockey player Kabir Khan, essayed by Shah Rukh Khan, is asked to quit the team. Years later, he is appointed coach of the women's hockey team, and the film follows the team and its coach on their journey to the top of the game–and the world.

A WALK DOWN THE STREET

In which we take you for a walk down Koni's streets:

'*Dreadful, gruesome, frightening. The world's largest slum. A disastrously overcrowded place where tens of thousands sleep in the streets, a hell of degradation and squalor, the cesspool of the world. A dying city. A vision of the end of man.*'

This was American journalist Peter T. White's recollection of Calcutta, published in the *National Geographic* magazine in 1973, two years prior to the publication of *Koni*. It is hard to imagine that two authors could come up with two such drastically different visions of the same city.

When Koni and Kshitish were walking down the streets of Calcutta, it is true that there were 55,571 pavement dwellers, and 5,500,000 people living in the 3000 slums that dotted the city, including Koni herself. The city was populated beyond its means, with 1,887,471 Bengali speakers, 286,684 Bihari migrants, 102,150 migrants from UP, roughly a million Muslims, over 33 lakh refugees from Bangladesh, 13,192 Tamilians, 40,985 Marwaris, who had made their way from Rajasthan, 20,000 native Anglo-Indians, nearly 5000 Chinese refugees, and many other communities that mingled to make the city.[1]

1. *Source: Calcutta Municipal Corporation records, Census of India, 1961, 1971*

As a by-product of its importance in the British Empire (as the nerve centre of its trade and the industrial hub of the East) the city had become increasingly attractive to migrant populations from all over the country. With the Partition of India, and later, the creation of Bangladesh the city was flooded by refugees from across the border. So, when Koni was walking down the streets around the fictitious Kamaldighi, Calcutta would have been teeming with people from all walks of life—a polluted and smoky city, because of all the factories that dotted it, and the fact that most of the cooking was done on charcoal chulahs or ovens.

Cityscape

The skyline of Calcutta was rapidly changing at the time. Old colonial buildings and the magnificent homes of upper-class Calcuttans were slowly giving way to highrises. Scaffolding was popping up all over the place, with ant-like builders and labourers climbing all over the façades. With the flagging-off of road construction everywhere, the streets were beginning to be dug up, causing traffic nightmares all over the city.

Transport

Public transport at the time was limited. The Calcutta Metro would not be running for about a decade. Calcutta's legendary tram system was the most popular mode of travel, and it was very well connected. The buses were mostly double-deckers, with steps at one end that led to the second tier. Taxis were not common as yet. Short distances were usually covered by hand-pulled rickshaws, which plied in most localities in the city.

Buses and trucks frequently held up traffic in the narrow lanes of the city. Pedestrian traffic was high, and mostly, walking was the quickest way to cover short distances. Sometimes, this too was treacherous, particularly in the monsoon season, when the streets tended to flood, and potholes were often left uncovered.

The River

The Hoogly River had always been the lifeblood of the city, right from when Job Charnock, an East India Company administrator and so-called 'founder' of Calcutta, united the three villages of Kalikata, Sutanati and Gobindopur (this claim has since been questioned by historians of the city). The port, located at Kidderpore, carried cargo all over the world. Calcutta was linked to its main railway station, located in the twin city of Howrah across the river, by the iconic Howrah Bridge. Launches (motorboats with open decks) ferried commuters at a nominal price. At leisure, a large number of Calcuttans would take joyrides on the river, on 20-foot long wooden country boats, punted by oarsmen using a long bamboo pole.

Entertainment

In the 70s television, had not yet become popular. For entertainment, Calcuttans would turn to the theatre, which were lively cultural hubs. It was a time of great political turmoil: the Emergency was about to be announced, and Calcutta was reeling under the Naxal insurrections. Bengali theatre reflected this, as plays started taking on increasingly political hues.

Bengalis have always been partial to reading and literature. College Street was the Mecca of book lovers, with its street-long parade of books. It still remains one of the largest market for secondhand books in the world.

The movies were also extremely popular. Great film-makers like Satyajit Ray, Ritwik Ghatak and Mrinal Sen called the city their home and inspiration. Cut-outs and painted movie posters dotted the Calcutta skyline. Long lines marked the release of most films, and tickets were sold in the black market with alarming regularity.

On most evenings, children would be greeted with the sound of the *dumroo* marking the arrival of the monkey trainers, who would travel all over the city with their dancing monkeys. Some of them even had domesticated bears that would perform for crowds. Snake charmers were also a common sight. The Bioscope-man was also a very popular figure among children. For as little as 10 paise, kids would crowd around the bioscope, watching pictures of their favourite movie stars and exotic locations on ancient projectors.

Food

The street food of Calcutta has always been special, and in the early 1970's, it was no different. Churan-wallahs were on every street corner wearing their trademark Nehru topis and selling their spicy-sweet digestive fare. The famous Calcutta specialty, puchka (golgappa) was ever popular. Nizam's had just started wrapping their kebabs in paranthas, kick-starting the kathi-roll phenomenon. Little stalls called 'cabins' served Mughlai paranthas (paranthas stuffed with eggs and meat) and kobiraji cutlets (meat, batter-fried with eggs). Some of these cabins specialized in kosha mangsho (a slow-cooked and sautéed mutton curry). Another favourite snack was the quarter pound of bread, toasted, buttered and sprinkled with sugar, usually served with tea.

The large immigrant Chinese Hakka community had been relocated to Tangra, on the outskirts of the city, where they set up many Chinese restaurants. But the old location of China Town, Tirreti Bazaar, in north-central Calcutta still served up hot Hakka fare all year round.

Mughlai restaurants were also very popular, especially those serving biryani, with its typical serving of meat, potato and eggs. Park Street was the hub of entertainment, and its restaurants, such as The Sky Room, Mocambo and Peter Cat were some of the city's favourite eateries. Of course, no neighbourhood in Calcutta would be complete without the local mishti (sweetmeats) shop. Rasagulla, sandesh, lal doi, nimki, lengcha, ladykeni, and many more were regularly served up. Most of these shops also offered kochuri-aloo, or kochuri-dal (a very popular stuffed puri served with either potatoes or dal) at breakfast and teatime.

SPORTS

As you would have gathered from reading *Koni*, Calcutta was particularly passionate about sports. Swimming clubs were founded wherever there was enough open water. Tanks, ponds and lakes, like Hedua (Kamaldighi from the story), College Square (adjacent to College Street), Padmapukur and Rabindra Sarobar had more than a few swimming clubs located on their waters. Akharas or gyms lined the city, where you could find bodybuilders, pehelwans, weightlifters and wrestlers training at all times of the day.

Rowing and golf were the sports of the elite, located mainly in south and central Calcutta. The Calcutta Race Course was the venue where thousands of people gathered on Sundays to watch the horse races and to gamble away lakhs of rupees.

Cricket, of course was already very popular in the city. The fortunes of the Bengal Ranji team as well as club cricket leagues were closely followed. The Eden Gardens was the home of Indian cricket, and had a reputation of very ardent and sometimes unruly fans, as seen in the riot-marred test matches against the West Indies and Australia in the 60's.

But Calcutta's true sporting passion was football. You must have heard of the traditional rivalry between Calcutta's two great football clubs, Mohun Bagan and East Bengal. Other clubs such as Mohammadan Sporting, Aryan, Wari and Tollygunge Agragami also vied for attention. Club loyalties were lifelong, and the matches were hard fought, not only amongst the players but also the spectators. On the day of an important game, parts of the city would be paralyzed as all traffic led to the hub of Indian football, the Maidan. Arguments and fights among the audience would often spill into the streets, depending on the outcome of the match, and violence often marred these games. But football was, and still is the number one sport in Calcutta.

Peter T. White's Calcutta, then, was very different from Koni, Kshitish, and Moti Nandy's Calcutta. There is no denying that the streets were overpopulated, dirty and smoky. There were thousands who lived on the streets and more who lived in terrible squalor. But Calcutta was also a city brimming with vibrancy, passion and triumph, much like Koni herself.

WHAT WOULD YOU HAVE DONE?

- ★ People like Binod Bhar (President of Jupiter Club, and present MLA) and Dhiren Ghosh (Secretary of Jupiter Club) are obviously trying to get you out of any position of power within the club. You have sacrificed a lot of sweat and blood for the club's cause, and have been training swimmers for years. They have not been performing up to the high expectations that you have set for them, and you are frustrated with them. They have alleged that your obsession is detrimental to the cause of winning medals. However, your loyalty to the club cannot be questioned, and you have been a lifelong member of Jupiter. In these circumstances, would you do as Kshitish Sinha did, and walk away from the club, and join Apollo? Or would you stick to the club that you have given so much to, and which has given so much to you in return?
- ★ You have a coach who is obsessed with making you win. Your whole life is being overtaken by this. Like Koni, you are being made to practise for hours. Your stamina is running low, and your will to continue is gone. You are almost in pain. But your coach, like Koni's, has promised to buy you something you really want (in Koni's case, the nylon swimming costume), and even

threatens you if you don't obey him. What would you do? Would you walk away from the session, tired of being pushed to your body's limits, or would you continue, knowing that not only is your coach pushing you towards victory, but also towards something you really want?

- ✯ Hiya, your future rival comes and offers you water when her teacher has already refused. You, like Koni, are convinced that you were refused it earlier because you looked poor, and the girls were from a rich people's school. What would you do in this situation? Be polite, and not let the incident bother you? Or would you react in anger, as Koni did?
- ✯ In Madras, Koni is accused of stealing Bela's cream. In fact, Hiya had used the cream, and put some on Koni's face. But Koni is slapped and branded a thief. When Hiya comes back, she dismisses the whole issue. But Koni who is angry, runs over to Hiya and slaps her across the face. In her mind, Bela hitting her was Hiya's fault. How would you deal with this ugly situation if you were subjected something similar? Would you blame Hiya, who had taken the cream in the first place, or Bela who obviously crossed a line, or not react at all, having been absolved of the allegations made against you?

★ You are Bishtu Dhar, of aristocratic lineage and hopeful of winning a seat in the Legislative Assembly. Kshitish Sinha and you start on the wrong note on the banks of the Ganga—he offends and insults you. Then, later, at a nonstop walking event, he interrupts your speech repeatedly. However, at the end of it, he offers you suggestions that transform your speech. You instantly spot his talent for speech-writing. In these circumstances, what would you do? Would you swallow your pride, and forgive the insults he has hurled at you for a 'larger' cause (your own gain)? Or would you ignore his skills and go on doing what you have been doing?

CHARACTER CLUES

★ I am not a small man. In fact, I weigh about 111 kilos. I come from an aristocratic lineage and I own several businesses in Burrabazar. I have a trusty 40-year-old Austin that takes me everywhere and I enjoy having various musical instruments being simulated on my body when I get a massage. My daily diet consists of 300 grams of kheer, fifteen luchis, twelve rotis at night, a quarter of a kilo of rice with four spoonfuls of ghee, and more. I plan to contest the next elections, but I need a good speech-writer by my side. Who am I?

★ I am a member of Jupiter Club, and claim to have represented India in the 1948 Olympics, in the 1500m category, as well as part of the water polo team. I missed the Bronze by point five of a second, and McLane, the American who won the gold said that the competition I gave him charged him up. Somehow Kshitish Sinha does not believe me, and keeps having a coughing fit in my presence. I do not like him and want him out of Jupiter. Who am I?

★ I am the coach of Ballygunge Swimming Club. One of my trainees is one of Koni's main rivals. But when Dhiren Ghosh starts using his usual dirty tactics to keep Apollo swimmers, and especially Koni, from the Bengal swimming team, I stand up for what is right, and refuse to allow any Ballygunge Swimming Club girls to participate if the team does not include Koni. Who am I?

★ My husband is a swimming coach, and I try and support his dreams of training a truly fantastic athlete, but I do not always understand his obsession. I want to start a tailoring shop, for which I have put up Rs. 5000 for the advance to my landlord, Bishtu Dhar. I do not particularly want to give Koni a job in my shop, but my husband convinces me to. Who am I?

★ I want the best for my family. If that means working non-stop for meagre pay, to be able to feed my mother and siblings, so be it. But my dream is to see my sister triumph against all odds. Maybe even go to the Olympics! But I am too sick to see this happen. Who am I?

★ I am the Maharashtra State girls' swimming champion, and I can swim the 100-metre in a minute and twelve seconds—a good eight seconds ahead of the average Indian girls swimming champion. Who am I?

★ I swim for Jupiter, and I am not a fair player. Two years ago, in my pre-university exams, I was caught cheating. I caused a scene by biting the guard who caught me. In the state championships, I block Koni, effectively ending the race for her. Who am I?

- ★ I had moved from Jupiter to Apollo because of coach Kshitish Sinha's excessive expectations. When he shifted to Apollo to train Koni, I went back to Jupiter. Khistish Sinha thinks I will never be able to compete at the highest level beause I am not committed and hardworking enough. In Madras, I don't perform well at the swimming events, and I also bicker with Hiya. This is my last year in competitive swimming as I am going to get married soon. Who am I?
- ★ I swim for the Ballygunge Swimming Club. I may be the fastest swimmer competing in women's swimming events in Calcutta. I come from a very privileged background. When I encounter Kshitish Sinha and Koni at the zoo, I offer them water, even though my teacher had refused them earlier. I love listening to music on the transistor. Who am I?

GLOSSARY

ALU CHHECHHKI A light potato curry, flavoured with mustard seeds

ALUKAABLIWALLAH A man who sells alukaabli. Alukaabli is a spicy potato dish or salad, made like a chaat

BARUNI A festival at the beginning of summer, when devotees of the goddess Ganga, offer thousands of raw mangoes to the river. It is traditional for children to go hunting for mangoes by jumping into the river

BOUDI Elder brother's wife or sister-in-law. Used informally to address older or married women

FOUR ANNAS Twenty-five paise

GAMCHHA Traditional chequered scarf, made from coarse cotton. Sometimes worn around the shoulder, it is used as a towel or to wipe sweat

LUCHI The Bengali version of the puri, made of flour and fried to puff up

PANCHPHORAN Traditional blend of five spices used in Bengali cooking, made by combining nigella seeds (kalonji), black mustard seeds, fenugreek seeds (methi), cumin seeds (jeera), and fennel seeds (saunf)

PRAJAPATI Butterfly

Rasagulla A sweet made of balls of cottage cheese cooked in sugar syrup

Singara Bengali samosas. The deep-fried, triangular outer shell is made of flour and stuffed with potatoes, green peas, lentil and coriander leaves. Many different fillings can be used

Telebhaja Deep fried pakoras or fritters. Vegetables are coated in gram flour and deep-fried

REVIEW THE BOOK

In which you decide how much you liked this book . . .

You have just finished reading Moti Nandy's *Koni*. One of the recurrent themes of Moti Nandy's work is the triumph of the underdog. Do you think this book reflects that?

What parts of the book related to you the most—the thrill of the races described in it, or the human story of the unlikely heroine?

Which characters spoke to you the most? Which characters did you not like?

Which parts were the most fun?

Think about the story. Which aspects would you change, and which ones would you leave alone?

Did you like the book? If so, why?

How do you rate this book?

Rate out of 10 stars.

* * * * * * * * * *